BAD THINGS HAPPEN
AT NIGHT

The shadowy organisation known as the Council of Thirteen has only one goal: to bring the full terror of Hell to Earth. But there is one thing stopping them — Archer, a young man who has been raised from birth to fight the Council and its minions every step of the way. Archer is given orders to hunt down and slay a mysterious killer who is terrorising Paris. Along the way, he learns a secret that his masters have been keeping from him . . .

DAVID WHITEHEAD

BAD THINGS HAPPEN AT NIGHT

Complete and Unabridged

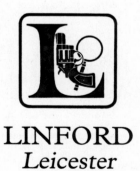

LINFORD
Leicester

First published in Great Britain in 2012

First Linford Edition
published 2013

A catalogue record for this book is available
from the British Library.

ISBN 978–1–4448–1727–0

Published by
F. A. Thorpe (Publishing)
Anstey, Leicestershire

Set by Words & Graphics Ltd.
Anstey, Leicestershire
Printed and bound in Great Britain by
T. J. International Ltd., Padstow, Cornwall

This book is printed on acid-free paper

For Angie Palmer.
All these demons for one little angel.

1

The demon's name was Milaroth, and he'd been trapped in this cold, stygian prison for what seemed like forever.

At first, when he'd finally realized the battle was lost, he had roared his defiance and hurled himself time and again at his invisible cage. He had been strong back then, but Tilonus's Binding Spells had been stronger; and by the time they had eventually weakened, so too had he.

Without the necessary nourishment to sustain him, he had been forced to watch his leathery body wither and shrink. Now, more than a century later, the only thing in him that still grew unchecked was his burning hatred for all Mankind.

More than a century later . . . ?

Had he *really* spent so long here in this near-complete darkness, struggling to break the Binding Spells, always without success?

He had no true idea, but he suspected

it was a century at least; a century, aye, and more. Unable to go forth as he once had, he could now only crouch here in his stinking nest, the home he had once been able to leave and return to at will.

He had had what seemed like eternity to sit and brood and plot — and watch himself grow ever weaker. At first he had beseeched his far-flung brothers — Ye'terel, Amorion and Skarasis — to come and rescue him. But he had known all along that rescue was impossible. The Ancient of the Ancients knew their craft well. Their spells and incantations were powerful and all but unbreakable.

But not . . . *quite.*

As the years went by, so Milaroth noticed that their spell-light, the near-undetectable glow that always lingered around anything magical, was no longer as bright as it had once been. Deep inside his dark, quasi-reptilian brain he realized that age was taking its toll on the spell, much as the elements eventually erode the mortar between bricks and in so doing weaken the whole.

It came to Milaroth then that the spell

would eventually weaken so that even he, in his now-pitiful state, should be able to shatter it once and for all.

And so he curled up in his nest with as much patience as he could muster . . . and waited.

Day after day he watched the spell-light. At first there seemed to be no further change in it. Sometimes it seemed to glow stronger, as if the very incantations that bound him there were themselves struggling to remain alive and potent.

But month after month, year after year, decade after decade, the light grew slowly, steadily fainter.

Unable to control his impatience, Milaroth sometimes tried to grab a strand of spell-light and snap it, to break the chain and thus break the spell. But the spell-light was to him as fire or acid would be to a human. It seared his gray flesh down to the very bone.

So he continued watching, and waiting.

Ironically, when the spell-light finally darkened perceptibly and then blinked out altogether, he didn't even see it happen. He was curled up in his nest, thinking dark, unthinkable thoughts of revenge and retribution.

The Ancient of the Ancients, the sect which had dedicated itself to the destruction of his kind, would pay dearly for what they had done to him. Because of their temerity, the rest of Mankind would suffer tenfold.

It was only then that he realized the spell-light had died.

That the spell *itself had* died.

That he was at last *free*.

With a low, rumbling growl Milaroth stirred hungrily in the darkness. He rolled up onto his feet with a soft scratching of claws against ice-cold stone. He straightened up and flexed wasted muscles and withered hands with ivory nails that looked more like fish-hooks.

He tested the darkness with almond-shaped eyes the color of congealed blood. The only sound was the rasp and saw of his hot breath, growing faster in time with his building excitement.

Finally he stepped forth — and met no resistance.

It was true, then! He really *was* free!

His dark mind swam with a million-times-a-million spite-filled thoughts. Revenge . . . retribution . . . but first —

First he needed . . . nourishment.

He moved slowly, purposefully, through the darkness. Around him, the dirt-smelling tunnel, the very warren he himself had excavated all those decades ago, was tight and crumbly, itself in an advanced state of decay. It slanted upward, then dipped, turned, and finally ended in some sort of barrier.

His large head cocked to one side, Milaroth ran a rough, exploratory palm across it and recognized the feel of bricks and mortar. He had been sealed in, then.

And bound by yet more spells?

He examined the darkness and smelled the cloying air with thick, flared nostrils. He could find no trace of further sorcery.

He brought his right arm back and made a fist. Scaly flesh stretched and rippled over ravaged muscle.

Then his arm blurred forward.

His horny knuckles punched a jagged hole through the wall as if the wall itself had been made of paper. Two bricks immediately jarred loose and fell outward to land with a splash in water on the far side.

At once Milaroth's snout wrinkled. Water. He had an instinctive dislike of it, as did most of his kind. And yet he knew the water here would not be deep, and because of that his mouth slowly worked itself into a semblance of a smile.

Again he punched the wall; again, again, using both clawed fists now, and feeding his declining strength with all those years of pent-up fury. Bricks tumbled from the wall, stench-filled water sprayed up around them, and faint streaks of dull, sepia-colored light began to make his almond-shaped pupils contract for the first time in more than a century.

At last he had a hole large enough to climb through.

Milaroth stepped down into filthy water that lapped around his scaly gray shins and calves. His breathing bounced back at him from the dim, stench-filled brick tunnel in which he found himself. All around him, fat brown rats squeaked in alarm and hurriedly scampered out of his reach. Most made it to safety. Many of the younger ones didn't, and those too close to him simply, suddenly, stopped living.

He looked down at their tiny, furred bodies, floating stiff and still on the surface of the water, and again his teeth showed in what was, for him, a smile of great satisfaction.

At length he examined his surroundings. Memory finally told him which direction he should take.

He wanted to rush now, but he was still too weak. So he moved on at the same tortuous pace, sometimes striding, sometimes staggering, until he came to a set of rusted rungs that were set into one of the tunnel's outward-curving walls.

He studied them for a moment, more memories rising sluggishly to the surface of his slowed, nourishment-starved brain. After a moment he remembered them, what he had used them for.

He reached for one of the rungs and began to climb.

At street level, a manhole cover moved slightly in its seating, then rose perhaps two or three inches and slid sideways with a cold, metallic grate of sound. Moonlight shone briefly on the patterned steel.

A few moments later something dark rose slowly, stealthily, out of the manhole.

Moonlight reflected off its gray, armored hide, off its long, brittle claws, off the sharp, curved teeth that showed when its cracked lips peeled back.

Milaroth slowly stood erect. He stared at the star-spattered sky and thought, *I am back, my brothers! I am free again!*

He smelled the night air. An uncountable number of odors assailed his broad nostrils, bringing with them still more memories. Everything looked different, of course, and yet he knew instinctively that these were still *his* streets, just as they had always been. And the children who occupied them . . . they were still as cattle to him.

He looked around. The city was aglow with light, but the hour was late and the broad, tree-lined streets were empty. To his left moonlight shimmered off the black, oily waters of the river. He knew Mankind no longer called it *Sequana*, as they had when he was very young, but he wondered if it was still known as the Seine.

Off to his right and some distance away rose some kind of large, brightly-lit tower, its iron girders crisscrossing each other like the strands in a spider's web as they climbed gracefully toward the purple sky. That was new, at least to him. He remembered construction of some kind, shortly before the Demon-Slayer had found him. This, he told himself, must have been what they were building at the time.

He wondered what it was, and what purpose it served.

And then —

'*Êtes vous affamé?*'

Milaroth stiffened, alarmed by the voice. He had never feared Mankind before. Why should he? But then he had known their limitations. He had no idea how dangerous they had become during his long incarceration.

'*Où allons-nous manger?*'

'*Pizza la Gourmandise?*'

'*Oui, bon.*'

He quickly slipped into cover behind some kind of wheeled vehicle, which had been parked at the curb nearby. His shadow, cast long and grotesque, showed what appeared to be a spine of sharp spikes and a thick, writhing tail.

The vehicle was new to him. He had never seen its like before, but he approximated it to some sort of horseless wagon with seats and windows.

From around a tree-lined corner on the other side of the street came a man and a woman of middle years, wearing long, thick coats against the late-night cold. Milaroth cocked his head slightly as, through one of the wagon's windows, he watched them hurry on their way, arm in arm, their steps clacking busily against the sidewalk, breath steaming from their open mouths.

They did not even think to glance across the street in his direction.

Milaroth watched them go. They

shaven-headed lamas who lived there the closest thing he'd ever had to family.

In their not-always-tender care he had been prepared for the day when he would go out into the world and do battle with the Council of Thirteen, a shadowy conclave of devils and demons whose sole aim was to establish a permanent gateway between Hell and Earth.

The Ancients had schooled him in all the main languages of the world so that he might go wherever he was needed and communicate with ease, and from the world's myriad religions had taught him spells and incantations both light and dark in order to destroy the evils he had been born to fight.

From the Ancients he had learned other, more physical kinds of combat, too — *Boabom*, which was primarily an art of self-defense, and *Lama Pai* and its derivatives, Tibetan White Crane and *Hop Gar*.

In every respect he had applied himself diligently and fulfilled the promise of his birthright, and in the process had satisfied even his most demanding teachers.

It was just a shame that it had all been a complete waste of time.

One day when he was about eight years old he had finally summoned the courage to ask ancient, bent-backed Narayan how he had come to end up at the monastery . . . and that was the day when everything — for him, at least — had changed.

It was, he had believed at the time, a simple enough question, but one that had often bothered him. Apart from anything else, he had known even at that tender age that he was different to the monks in almost every physical respect. He was blue-eyed, *round*-eyed, and his hair was sandy blond. He stood tall even then and knew he would eventually grow taller still and dwarf the squatly-built monks.

Where, then, had he come from?

Narayan, a shrunken little dwarf with a face wrinkled like overripe fruit, had said in his soft, fractured voice, 'Why do you ask, child?'

'Because I am different,' he had replied.

'We are all different, child. No two are

ever exactly the same.'

'That's not what I mean.'

'Then what *do* you mean?'

Archer had hesitated then, as he struggled to find the right words to describe exactly how he felt. Finally he said, 'There's something in me that is . . . missing. Something that has *always* been missing.'

Narayan's reaction was an infinitesimal lifting of wispy eyebrows. 'Oh?'

'I don't know what it is,' explained the boy. 'Only that I have never truly known the inner peace you have tried to teach me. I have always felt . . . ' he shrugged, ' . . . incomplete, somehow. As if I do not really *belong*.'

'You are that rarest of all gifts, child,' said Narayan, after a moment. 'You are the seventh son of the seventh son of the seventh son, and as such the most powerful weapon we have against the Council of Thirteen. You are bound to feel the weight of such a burden.'

But that didn't really answer the question, so the child tried to come at his problem from a different direction.

'Narayan,' he asked. 'What were my parents like?'

To his surprise Narayan said, 'That I do not know, child.'

Archer gawped at him. 'But you have been here forever!' he blurted. 'Did you never see them when they first brought me here?'

Narayan's expression had shown discomfort then. But no one at the monastery ever lied, so the old man told the truth without hesitation. 'They did not bring you, child. We *took* you from them.'

The boy was stunned. '*Took* me? You mean . . . *stole* me?'

'Aye,' Narayan confirmed regretfully, 'and this we did with a heavy heart. But we knew they would never give you over to us willingly, no matter how special you were or how great our need. And our need was and remains so great that we had no choice.'

Archer was silent for a long moment. Then:

'Where did I come from, Narayan?'

'Is it really so important to know, child?'

What he saw in the lad's troubled azure eyes was answer enough.

'From a land far from here, called America,' said the old man at last. 'But enough questions. The past is done and cannot be *un*done. We are your guardians now, and *this* is your life, your destiny. It is better for you to accept it than to fight it.'

It was, as usual, sage advice. But try as he might, Archer had been *unable* to accept it. That night he had curled up in his bed with a million new questions for company. What were his parents like? Had they been *good* people? How had they felt when he was stolen away from them?

There in the absolute blackness of the freezing Tibetan night, he could almost feel the pain of their loss — and his own.

Clearly he had siblings out there somewhere; at least six brothers and perhaps even a sister or two he would never, ever know. And that in turn raised perhaps the most compelling question of all.

What kind of life would he have lived had he not been the seventh son of the seventh son of the seventh son?

Certainly less lonely than the one he lived now.

He thought of his upbringing by the crop-headed, red-robed nuns, who had raised him in an efficient and businesslike manner and taught him language and mathematics, philosophy and meditation, debate, ritual, chanting, art and the practices of the Buddha.

They had done all that, and done it well, but they had never *cared* for him. And though he never fully understood why, he had always craved their affection. To them, however, he had never been more than a commodity — a precious one, it was true, but no more than a means to an end.

He decided he had had enough of it.

With the reckless impetuosity of youth, he decided he would run away and find his real family. Only then would he really know a sense of completion, and love. He didn't know how he would accomplish the task, but he knew absolutely that he would — until the reality of his situation soon intruded.

18

He was but a child in a vast and inhospitable land. Even supposing he could escape from the monastery, where would he go? The only real choice was south, to Lhasa, with its wandering river and fortress-like Potala Palace complex. But the lamas would know that, and catch him long before he reached that far distant metropolis.

Besides, even at that young age his education had already been fully-rounded. He knew he wouldn't get far as a young boy travelling alone. He knew he would need money if he were to find some way to leave Tibet and travel to this faraway land called America.

He concluded — grudgingly — that there was only one sensible course open to him: to wait for the day when the lamas finally sent him out into the world.

For that day he waited another thirteen years.

And now here he was, twenty-one years of age, with a passport that would take him to practically any place on earth, a China Eastern Airlines ticket which had brought him to Paris, and a bank account from which he could draw funds as and when he needed them.

The Ancients had sent him here for a specific purpose, but he had no intention of carrying it out. As far as he was concerned, Paris was just a stepping-stone from one life into another.

Archer was heading for America . . . and as far as he was concerned, the rest of the world could take care of itself.

★   ★   ★

At last the taxi pulled up outside the Hotel Vernes, which was a bland, modern-looking structure seven stories high. Archer climbed out and swung his only item of luggage, a canvas cross-body bag, up and over one muscular shoulder. As he did so it clipped a tall, lean black man who was just passing behind him.

The black man staggered a little, then righted himself. He appeared to be in his late fifties, with a well-defined face beneath a black leather Kangol cap. Archer immediately said, '*Excusez-moi, m'sieur.*'

But the black man only frowned at him. '*Was war das?*' he demanded.

Archer automatically switched to German. '*Ich sagte, entschuldigung Sie mich.*'

Still black man scowled at him. '*Io non vi capisco.*'

Without thinking, Archer said in Italian, '*Mi dispiace mi sono imbattuto in voi.*'

The black man shook his head impatiently. 'Sorry, Champ,' he said at last, his voice deep and well-modulated, his accent clearly American. 'I don't have a *clue* what you' tryin' to say.'

This time it was Archer's turn to frown. He was just about to switch to English when, behind him, the taxi driver said pointedly, 'That will be forty-three Euros, m'sieur.'

Archer glanced down at him. '*Juste un instant, s'il vous plait.*'

He turned back to the black man . . .

. . . but the black man was no longer in sight.

Immediately on his guard, Archer scanned the wide pavement in front of the hotel but could see no trace of the man among the other passers-by.

'*M'sieur?*' said the taxi driver.

A skin-tingling sense of unease suddenly overtook him. Maybe he hadn't been as clever as he'd supposed. Maybe the lamas had somehow divined his true intentions all along and sent someone to keep an eye on him.

Or . . .

Or maybe the Council of Thirteen had somehow discovered that he was coming, and the black man had been one of their emissaries.

If there was one thing he had learned over the years, it was that evil could take many guises.

'*M'sieur?*' the taxi driver repeated impatiently.

Archer turned back, gave the driver a bright gold fifty-euro note and then headed for the hotel.

3

Still keeping a watchful eye on his surroundings, he entered the lobby and booked in. The way he carried himself was light and effortless, as if he were more perfectly-crafted machine than man. He made no sound and caused no stir — everything about him was fluid, easy.

Emotionally, however, it was a different story. The elevator took him up to a modest but comfortable room on the fifth floor, where he set his bag down in one corner, then finally allowed himself to sag a little.

Slowly, dispiritedly, he walked across to the facing, wall-length window. His reflection showed him the tall, compact young man he had become, with curly, nape-length blond hair, a long, boyish but vaguely troubled face and inescapably sad eyes.

He had cause to feel troubled.

The Ancients had prepared him for almost every eventuality except going out into the world for the first time, and interacting with the people who occupied it. Aside from occasional trips into Lhasa, the bulk of his life had been spent within the monastery's peaceful, weather-worn walls, and now he felt hopelessly adrift, almost embarrassingly naïve . . . truly a stranger in a strange land.

Beyond the glass, Paris was a cluttered jumble the like of which he had never seen before. After the calm serenity of his homeland, of the Lulang and Nyingtri forests with their smell of clustered cypress trees, the shallow valleys and tiny lakes and incalculably old mountains where the snow never thawed, the pace of life he now saw below him was almost impossible to grasp, much as it had been when he first arrived in Chengdu.

It was all going to take some getting used to.

He closed his eyes, squared his shoulders and allowed himself to feel each vertebra settle gently on top of the one beneath it. He relaxed his arms and legs and focused on the rhythmic flow of his breathing.

In his mind he pictured the monastery, perched high on a rugged hill sprinkled with rhododendron and primula, snow lotus and pedicularis.

The monastery . . .

It encompassed almost 250,000 square meters. Within its walls stood a massive, four-storey pagoda surrounded by smaller but no less impressive structures, each one constructed in an age beyond memory. Among these structures was a meeting hall built hard against the southwest corner, with a large square of packed dirt before it.

Stone steps led up to a grand entrance flanked by statues of Buddha. He pictured himself climbing them now, one, two, three, four . . .

Inside was housed a collection of precious *sutras*, or sermons, dating back to the Qing Dynasty, and statues of Tsong Khapa, Kwan-yin Bodhisattva, Man-jushri Bodhisattva, Amitayus, and Jamyang Qoigyi.

It had always been a place of the utmost peace and tranquility, and he had never felt calmer than when he was safe within its mural-painted walls.

Gradually his doubts and insecurities began to fade, and perspective once again asserted itself.

He opened his eyes once more.

Among other things, the lamas had trained him to acquire and accumulate a vast array of information. Now he searched his memory for the population of Paris. At the last estimate it had stood at close to two and a quarter million people.

It should be easy to drop out of sight here, he thought.

But a country's population could work against him, too. The population of America, for example, presently stood at more than three *hundred* million. What chance did he really have of finding his birth family in a land of so many?

And yet it might not be as impossible as it seemed. To begin with, his abduction twenty-one years earlier must have been reported at the time. If he could only find a reference to it on the internet or in the dusty back-issues of some provincial newspaper, his quest would be simplified considerably.

Of course, he had yet to figure out how to actually *use* the internet.

But even if that failed . . . well, he knew he was looking for a large family, and his name — he had never known any other — might also be a clue. Perhaps *Archer* had been his family's last name. Or perhaps it signified his star-sign — that he was Sagittarian, born between November 22 and December 21.

These clues might not sound like much, but at the very least they might help him narrow his search a little.

So it was with a sense of cautious optimism that he stared out over the city, his eyes finally tracing the graceful lines of the Eiffel Tower, as it reached up to skewer the scudding gray clouds to the south with its single steel arm.

And that was when a voice behind him said, 'Impressive, isn't it, Champ?'

★　★　★

Archer wheeled around, stunned that anyone could have entered the room so silently, and as he did so he instinctively dropped into a balanced, defensive position that was so typical of the long-fist, no-nonsense style of *Hop Gar*.

The speaker — the same black man he'd encountered outside — grinned broadly, revealing straight, well-set teeth. Speaking in fluent Mandarin this time he said, 'You're Archer.'

His expression showed just how much he was enjoying Archer's surprise.

Archer's fists tightened still further. 'Who are you?' he asked, matching the black man's choice of language.

'I'm Palden.'

Archer ran the name through his mind, but it meant nothing to him.

'It translates as 'Glorious One',' the black man added helpfully.

'Is that supposed to impress me?' asked Archer.

'Maybe not now,' the black man replied with a shrug, 'but it will. See, I'm here to *help* you, Champ. So best you treat me with a little respect, okay?'

Archer studied the other man closer. Palden stood a lean but muscular six feet. He had incisive caramel-colored eyes above high cheekbones, a broad nose and a wide mouth. He wore a soft silver sport coat over a tropical print shirt worn outside a pair of white sateen cotton trousers, and sneakers like his own. On any other man of his age the combination would have looked ludicrous. On Palden it looked unbelievably stylish.

Furthermore, he could sense no evil in the man.

Archer pondered Palden's seemingly guileless expression and again wondered if the Ancients had seen through him after all; that they had known all along what he'd been planning to do the minute they gave him his freedom.

Was that why this man Palden was here? To *stop* him?

Deciding that it would be wise to know his enemy, Archer said carefully, 'All right. Sit down.'

'*That's* more like it.'

Palden took off his Kangol cap, revealing a completely shaven head, and

29

without even seeming to look, flicked the cap carelessly toward the hook on the back of the door. It caught and stayed there.

Palden himself, meanwhile, went directly to the bed, hopped lightly onto it and stretched out, his sneakered feet crossed at the ankles, his long, manicured fingers laced at the nape of his neck.

'How did you get in here?' asked Archer.

Palden grinned. 'It's neat, right? The way I just show up like that?'

'Not really.'

'Aw, come *on*, now! Where's your sense of humor, buddy? You have *got a* sense of humor, haven't you? You'll need one in this business, trust me.'

'I've got one,' Archer replied stiffly, not at all sure that he really did. 'I just don't see that there's anything funny about someone breaking into my room, that's all.'

'Well, I'd hardly call it *that*.'

'Maybe *you* wouldn't. But why couldn't you just knock, like a normal person?'

'Because we're *not* normal people, Champ.' Palden treated him to a sudden scowl, then shook his head.

'What's wrong?' Archer asked defensively.

'Nothin'.'

'Come on, out with it.'

'Jus' thinkin', is all,' said Palden.

'About . . . ?'

'About how Demon-Slayers ain't what they used to be,' Palden replied bluntly.

Despite his training, Archer felt an uncharacteristic stab of anger. 'And what would *you* know about it?'

'Champ, I wasn't much older than you are now when the Ancients sent me out into the big wide world with orders to stop the Thirteen wherever and whenever I found 'em. But I don't remember ever lookin' as green as you do right now. Inside I always felt . . . more *mature*, somehow.'

Archer's eyes narrowed. 'Are you telling me you're a Demon-Slayer, too?'

'You didn't think you were the only one, did you?' Palden shook his head again. 'We're rare. I mean, the seventh son of the seventh son of the seventh son doesn't come along every day of the week. But when they *do*, the Ancients . . . ' he trailed off, searching for the right word.

'They *abduct* us,' Archer replied venomously.

Palden made no attempt to deny it. 'Yep,' he agreed cheerfully. 'They steal us away and raise us to fight the Thirteen, 'cause there's no other way. We're the only weapons they got.'

'But that doesn't make it right,' Archer said bitterly. 'Who gives them the power to take us away from our families and deprive us of a life?'

'We *have* a life, Champ. We *make* a life, when we go out into the world.'

'You mean we can date, and marry, and raise families and get mortgages?'

Palden cocked his head curiously. 'Is that what you *want*, Archer?'

'I don't know,' Archer replied honestly. 'But it would've been nice to have had the choice.'

'It sure would,' said Palden. 'But we didn't — so get over it and do your damn job.'

'I'll do my job, don't worry,' Archer said testily, and he hated the feeling he got when he said it — when he lied.

'But I *do* worry,' said Palden, sitting up again. 'Everyone involved in this battle worries when a new Demon-Slayer goes out into the world for the first time, 'cause he can go one of two ways. He can take risks and make mistakes and get himself killed because he's so all-fired eager to prove himself . . . or he can figure to hell with this and jus' take off.'

'I don't know what you're talking about,' said Archer.

'Oh, come off it, Champ. It's written all over your pretty young face. But not 'cause you're scared.'

'Well, you're right about that. I'm *not.*'

'Too bad. Only a fool knows no fear.'

'How profound,' Archer said witheringly.

'Not really. I heard it one time on *Star Trek: The Next Generation.* But it's true, Champ. Believe me.'

'So what's my problem, then?' demanded Archer. 'If it's not fear?'

'You're pissed,' Palden said simply.

'Pissed at the Ancients for pluckin' you from your crib and raisin' you the way they did. I don't blame you. But they didn't do it just for the exercise. This is *serious* stuff, Champ.'

'I know that. It's all I've *ever* known. But you don't have to worry about me. I'll get the job done.'

Palden reached into his jacket and took out a packet of cigarettes.

'What are you doing?' asked Archer, startled.

'What does it look like I'm doin'?'

'Those things are — '

' — bad for me, sure,' finished Palden. 'But what can you do? You live among these people long enough, you pick up some of their bad habits . . . especially if you want to blend in.'

'Well, you've certainly done a good job of *that*.'

'Don't knock it till you've tried it, Champ. You do your job and do it right, you've got a lot to look forward to between assignments.' Without warning he grinned hugely. 'I mean, jus' wait till you do the *wild* thing.'

'The wild thing?'

'You know — bump fuzzies. Hit a home run. Partake of a little horizontal refreshment.' He saw the look of incomprehension on Archer's face and shook his head pityingly. 'Take ol' one-eye to the optometrist,' he said very deliberately.

Archer finally got it. 'That's disgusting,' he said, blushing.

'You won't say that after you've tried it,' Palden assured him. He fired up a cigarette and sobered suddenly. 'But that's for the future — assumin' you live long enough to *have* one. For now, let's jus' concentrate on what's brought you here, Champ.'

He went on, 'Somethin' broke into Clinique de la Mère on Rue de Monttessuy two nights ago. By the time it left again twelve newborn babies, all the babies in the hospital at the time, were dead. There wasn't a mark on them, nothin' to suggest how they died, or why they all died within minutes of each other. An' you're here to find out why.'

'The Ancients already *know* why,' Archer replied. 'In 1887, a Demon-Slayer named Tilonus fought a demon named Milaroth no more than a kilometer or two from the hospital. Milaroth was a demon who drew his life-force from — '

' — from the souls of the newborn and the young,' Palden finished, making an impatient rolling motion with his right hand to hurry the conversation along. 'I know my demons, Champ. Go on.'

'Well, because Tilonus was old by then, he no longer had the strength to actually *slay* Milaroth. The best he could manage was to use spells to imprison him in his nest.'

'So the Ancients believe the spells might have finally reached the end of their life.'

'Exactly.'

'And the first thing Milaroth did when they gave up altogether was go out an' snack on some nice, fresh baby-souls, right?'

This time it was Archer's turn to scowl. 'Are you *sure* you're a Demon-Slayer, Palden?'

'Don't ever doubt it, Champ.'

'It's just that I was always taught the

sanctity of human life, and respect for the dead.'

Palden blew smoke. 'Listen up, kid,' he said, rising. 'I've been around a *long* time. Sometimes I think *too* damn' long. What I've seen, what I've experienced, some of the things I've had to do . . . it's enough to make even a Demon-Slayer cynical. Besides — '

'What?'

'Forget it. You'll learn in your own sweet time. So — where do you think you'll find Milaroth?'

'I'm going to track him back from the clinic.'

'Why not just go straight to Port Debilly?'

'Port Debilly . . . ?'

'The site of his original banishment?'

'I know what I'm doing, believe me.'

'I never said you didn't, Champ, I just asked *why.*'

'Because there's no guarantee he'll still be there.'

'He'll be there, all right,' said Palden. 'For more than a century he's been starved of the one thing that gives him his power. Twelve babies aren't enough to restore him to full strength. He'll need to feast again and again before he returns to anything like his former self — and has the energy to move on and build a new nest elsewhere.'

Archer saw the logic to that but stubbornly refused to admit it. 'I'll do it my way,' he said.

'Sure, knock yourself out. But remember this, Champ. He knows you're comin'. Somehow the Thirteen will have forewarned him. And now that he's fed, even a little, he'll be a whole lot stronger than he was.'

'I'll remember that,' said Archer, turning back to the window and the panorama beyond, 'just before I slay him.'

Behind him he heard Palden snort. 'You' gonna track him down and slay him just like that, huh?'

'Just like that, yeah.'

'Well, good luck with it, Archer. I got a feelin' with your attitude you might need it.'

Irritated, Archer heeled back around. 'Thanks for the — '

But there was no longer any sign of Palden. Even his Kangol cap had vanished from the hook on the back of the door.

Archer was the room's sole inhabitant.

4

As wintry darkness spilled across Paris, news crews from a dozen different countries finally decided to call it a day and in ones and twos drove their vans away from the impromptu camp they'd set up outside Clinique de la Mère.

The story of the dead babies had shocked the world. The chances of a dozen babies in the same location all suffering some form of cot death or apnea within seconds of each other was as close to impossible as it was possible to get. But what else did that leave?

Staff had been interrogated, their backgrounds investigated, their mental health evaluated urgently but meticulously. Equipment — incubators, monitors, infant warmers and more — had been checked, rechecked and found to be in perfect working order. Charts were examined, blood tests taken, autopsies performed, theories proposed. But still no one could explain why twelve seemingly healthy babies had, one after another, simply died.

And yet *something* had snuffed out those twelve innocent lives. And where it had happened once, who was to say it wouldn't happen again, somewhere else; later today, perhaps, or tomorrow, or the day after?

Paris was gripped by fear and unease, and that same mixture of emotions was felt by the parents of newborn babies the world over.

A short distance from the hospital, Archer waited for the last of the press vans to leave, then stepped soundlessly from the shadows of a boutique doorway.

He hadn't really intended to come here at all, of course. The airport, and America, had been his intended destination. But he had decided that it might be best to at least make a *pretence* of investigating the matter, just in case Palden was still keeping an eye on him.

And Archer *was* being watched, he could feel it.

The clinic was a smart, ultra-modern

41

building surrounded by a textured red-brick wall. Beyond the wall the tops of stunted ornamental trees hinted at the pleasant, sculpted grounds beyond.

A cold breeze picked up but Archer, who had been taught from infancy to regulate his temperature according to his surroundings, was oblivious to it.

Instead — and really just for the exercise, or so he tried to convince himself — he scanned the perimeter wall closely, searching for any lingering psychic aura that might allow him to pick up Milaroth's trail.

After a few minutes he sensed more than saw a thin, spidery track running up over the outer wall. It would be invisible to anyone who was either not sufficiently sensitive or who had not been trained to recognize the distinctive spoor demons left to mark their passing.

It also confirmed that the Ancients had been right in their suspicions. Milaroth, the so-called Feaster-on-Newborn-Souls, had indeed escaped his place of exile and once again walked the earth.

Archer glanced from left to right.

Although the feeling of being watched persisted, the street was apparently empty.

He ran lightly toward the wall, sprang up, grabbed its ridge and swung himself nimbly onto its narrow top.

Then he froze, as if someone had suddenly pressed life's *Pause* button.

A black-clad man with a long-barreled pump-action Remington 870 shotgun tucked in close to his side was making a perfunctory check of all the shadows and shrubbery directly beneath him.

Holding his breath, Archer looked down at him. The man's combat uniform and golden insignia identified him as an officer of *La Jaune*, France's Mobile Gendarmerie, whose responsibility it was to maintain security in and around public buildings.

Silently, Archer berated himself. He should have known that the clinic would have been put under some kind of surveillance and protection. The same thing was probably happening in and around every hospital in the country.

Fortunately, the gendarme had no

inkling of Archer's presence immediately above him. He satisfied himself that this particular section of the grounds was intruder-free, then slowly moved on.

Archer dropped lightly as a feather to the ground behind him. He crouched for a time, waiting, listening, scanning the darkness for a sign of the policeman's companions. He spotted three of them. They did not spot him.

When he was satisfied that he had noted the positions of all the gendarmes, he shifted his gaze to better examine the rear elevation of the building.

Almost immediately he spotted a faintly-glowing trail running crookedly up toward the hospital's flat roof.

As distasteful as it was, it was easy to imagine what had happened after Milaroth had gained access to the sleeping medical center from above, and then worked his way cautiously downstairs.

He would have entered the maternity unit, bending to pass through the doorway, and then had to do nothing more sinister than stride from one end of the ward to the other. In his wake the babies to either side of him would have simply ceased to stir, or twitch, or gurgle contentedly . . . or breathe.

Through some dark form of osmosis he would have drawn their souls from them, converted them into pure nourishment, and then absorbed them, leaving only empty husks in his wake.

The shiver that ran through Archer had nothing to do with the weather. He was thinking about the sense of loss the parents of each dead child had been forced to suffer, and wondering if his own parents had suffered similar agony when their own child had been taken from them.

The idea of walking away from all this, of traveling to America in search of his lost family, was suddenly stronger than ever. But almost before he knew it, he was slipping noiselessly from the bushes and circling the hospital, studying every elevation for the trail that would show him where Milaroth had left after feasting.

When he reached the opposite side of

45

the clinic he caught the faintest trail meandering down across walls and windows like the glistening ooze some gigantic slug might leave behind it.

He sprang noiselessly at the tall, padlocked side-gates and more or less vaulted them, landing on the far side with barely a stir.

The trail came down into the hospital parking lot and then across the street toward Avenue de la Bourdonnais.

Grimly, Archer followed it.

It wasn't easy. Three days had passed and the inclement weather ensured that the faint aura was degrading by the moment.

Archer moved swiftly along the narrow, tree-lined street, past small stores and restaurants until he reached Quai Branly. He turned left, stopped, scanned the broad thoroughfare that paralleled the Seine and finally detected a thin, faint glow that told him he was still on the right track.

Light traffic passed in both directions as he continued to ghost along beneath trees now almost bare of blossom. To his left the Eiffel Tower stood sentinel over the city, lit in bright shades of yellow and gold that, in the darkness, made it look more like a launched rocket frozen halfway to heaven.

When he reached the landmark the trail, all but completely faded now, led him right, across Pont d'Ilena. He crossed the bridge with the absolute conviction that he was closing in on his prey. To left and right the river glistened black and restless, sluggish like crude oil. Moored boats fidgeted in the swell.

Archer stopped again at the corner where the Pont d'léna fed out onto wide, neon-lit . . .

He felt a sudden rush of irritation.

Port Debilly.

Exactly where Palden had said he'd find Milaroth.

Archer looked right and saw nothing of note. But a manhole cover about twenty meters to his left seemed to catch the light briefly when he glanced that way.

Cautiously, he strode down toward it. Traffic was getting lighter by the minute now, and the squally weather was keeping all but the hardiest pedestrians off the streets.

Shielded from the occasional traffic by a line of parked cars and trees, he crouched beside the manhole and gently set one palm down on the cold, patterned metal.

Immediately he drew his hand away, as if from a naked flame.

There was something almost unutterably evil beneath that cover.

This, then, really *was* the site of the original banishment.

There were two thin slits in the manhole to facilitate its lifting and removal. Still not really knowing why he didn't just turn around and walk away, Archer reached down toward them and was just about to wrench the manhole from its mooring when a voice behind him said, 'You, there! What are you doing?'

⋆   ⋆   ⋆

Archer froze, then slowly turned his head.

A pale-faced, dark-haired girl of about

48

his own age was standing a short distance behind him, watching him through near-black, scared eyes. She wore a buttoned-to-the-throat navy blue pea jacket over skinny-leg jeans and ankle boots. Her raven-black hair, which she wore to shoulder-length, fell in waves from beneath a gray retro driving cap.

He wondered where she'd come from and how to answer her. But before he could say anything at all she asked in an anxious hiss, 'Did you see it, too? That night?'

He slowly straightened back up. 'See what?' he asked innocently.

Instead of answering, she only offered another question. 'You've been following it from the clinic, haven't you?'

She spoke quietly, her voice not much more than a whisper, and every so often her eyes darted nervously toward the manhole cover behind him.

'I don't know what you're talking about,' he said.

'You *do*,' she countered, her fear suddenly morphing into anger. 'I can see it in your face.'

'Who *are* you?' he asked.

'My name is — '

The manhole cover suddenly exploded up out of the ground and something large and gray reared up behind Archer, roaring loud enough to burst his eardrums.

Before he could react, Milaroth — for it could be none other — leapt up out of the hole and yanked him off his feet.

Archer had one fleeting glimpse of the demon's face — almond-shaped eyes that were a dull, muddy red, a gray snout wrinkled now in a snarl full of spite, a sudden blast of fetid breath that made him want to be sick — and then Milaroth threw him across the pavement.

Archer hit the flagstones hard and slammed up against the waist-high railings beyond which lay the river. Somewhere to his right he heard the girl scream. It stopped him from blacking out altogether.

As he scrambled back to his feet, the demon reached down for the fallen manhole cover, moving impossibly fast for something so large that must still be so relatively weak.

Archer's breath locked in his throat.

Milaroth was tall, broad of shoulder, his skin scaly and armored like that of a rhinoceros.

Then he lifted the manhole cover as if it were no more than a paper plate and hurled it at Archer.

Archer threw himself aside a second before it smashed into the railings with a heavy clang, denting the metal poles and chipping their cream-colored coating of paint.

Not giving him a second, Milaroth growled and came charging toward him, the spikes that traced his deep-set spine flexing and rippling, his tail whipping and snapping as if in anticipation of the killing to come.

Archer, his mind suddenly a jumble, came up and forced himself to let instinct to take over.

He whipped around, his left leg shot out and the blade of his foot crashed against the demon's inner thigh. Taken by surprise, Milaroth stumbled slightly; almost matching him in speed, Archer spun back the opposite way, brought his left leg around in a hooking motion that caught Milaroth behind the knee, and brought him forward and down.

As soon as the demon's head was within range, Archer punched him a hard roundhouse to the horny ridge of bone that was his left ear. The blow hurt Archer more than it did his opponent.

Milaroth growled and lashed out at him, his tail suddenly flicking faster than ever. Archer danced back and then came in again almost immediately, his hands still moving, but now describing weird, arcane patterns in the air before the demon as he prepared to speak the incantation that would slay him.

Milaroth powered back up onto his feet, snatched at Archer, caught him, hoisted him easily overhead — and threw him.

Archer sailed right over the railings and plunged down toward the icy waters of the Seine.

The last thing he heard was the dark-eyed girl, still screaming.

5

For a shockingly short time Archer fell through the chilly darkness, bracing himself for the inevitable plunge into ice-cold water.

Then he landed with a thud against something hard.

Pain tore through his ribs and he groaned, then rolled onto his side. Dimly he realized he'd landed on the roof of a moored pleasure boat. He thrust up onto his knees, the boat yawing drunkenly beneath his weight, and shook his head to clear it.

Somewhere above him, the girl screamed again.

Archer sprinted across the top of the boat and leapt down onto the jetty beside it. The jetty was a steel pontoon — it also dipped beneath him and, not expecting it, he stumbled, all his earlier grace suddenly deserting him.

Teeth clamped together, he fairly threw

himself at the ramp at its far end, which led up to street level, knees and arms pumping effortlessly, his only thoughts now for the girl and her safety.

Above him, a long, ominous growl filled the night.

A locked gate barred the way ahead. He jumped, caught the bars and threw himself up and over with hardly a pause. He came down light on the other side, knees bent to absorb the landing, then twisted at the waist to locate the demon he intended to kill and the girl he intended to save.

The girl, he saw, had made a run for it. Even above the rush of blood in his ears he could hear the clacking of her shoes as she tried to distance herself from the thing that meant to kill her.

But Milaroth had no intention of allowing that to happen. He wasn't running; there was no need for that. His long, intent strides were eating up the ground faster than the fastest sprinter.

Archer saw the girl cast one pale-faced look back over her shoulder, knowing that this contest could have only one outcome.

But not if he could help it.

He powered up into a full-out run that had to be seen to be believed. A cheetah never moved more gracefully as he ate up the distance, the muscles in his arms bunching in readiness for the coming confrontation.

He was perhaps six meters behind Milaroth, and Milaroth was certainly no more than three meters behind the girl, when the demon suddenly became aware of his presence.

Without warning Milaroth stopped in his tracks and spun around; and Archer, reacting quicker than thought, immediately fell forward into a roll that took him beneath his opponent's questing claws.

He came up into a crouch and with everything he had in him punched Milaroth hard between the legs.

It was like punching steel.

Archer sucked back a cry and quickly scrambled on between the demon's legs, shaking and flexing his hand to bring some feeling back into it.

Before the demon could turn and face him he grabbed its tail — it was like thick rope and he could feel a sickly, rhythmic wash of blood pulsing through it.

He threw himself back between the demon's legs and wrenched with all the strength in him, and Milaroth slammed over onto his back with a roar that was almost indignant.

At once Archer leapt on him, hoping his weight, slight as it was, would crack the demon's sternum or cause some other injury that would incapacitate, and give him the chance to cast the spell required to slay.

With a snarl Milaroth rolled away at the last moment and Archer came down on stone, not flesh, and pain jagged through his ankles.

He chanced to take his eyes off Milaroth for a second, and saw with a sinking feeling that the girl had stopped to watch the contest instead of taking advantage of the time he was buying her.

Then Milaroth hit him.

It was a vicious punch that would have sheared the head off a lesser man. Even so, the force of it slammed Archer into a nearby tree and the tree actually shook, its branches rattling, with the impact.

Before he could recover, Milaroth grabbed him by the shoulders and tossed him back toward the railings. Archer sailed over them, pitched down into the Seine and this time he *did* hit the water, and worse than that . . . the water hit him right back.

★ ★ ★

As he struck the glistening surface the water smacked him in the face, the hands, the arms, the body, the legs and feet, and he blacked out momentarily.

When consciousness returned a second or two later he realized his mouth and nose were already filling with water, that he was drowning, and he forgot all his training and began to panic.

Palden was right, he thought. He *was* green. He didn't have the sense to know the true meaning of fear and the life-saving caution that fear could inspire. And yes, he *had* stupidly tried to prove himself, if only to get Palden off his back. And the only place it had gotten him was —

Suddenly he broke the surface, coughing up water, gasping for air, splashing wildly as if he'd forgotten every swimming lesson he'd ever had.

Around him the night seemed darker somehow, the water thicker and inkier. He thought he felt something beneath the surface touch his leg and immediately called to mind everything he'd ever learned about the demons of the depths — of Rahab and Kraken, Leviathan, the Hydra and all their hideous brethren. He resisted the urge to kick out. It was imagination, that was all, he was losing focus just like the inexperienced kid he was —

Above him, another long, ominous growl brought him back to the here and now. As he looked up again he saw the girl climbing awkwardly over the railings. Outlined against the cloudy night sky, she wobbled briefly and quickly held her gloved hands out for balance.

Helpless for the moment, Archer could only watch as Milaroth suddenly appeared behind her and reached one massive, taloned claw out to snag her shoulder.

'*Jump!*' yelled Archer.

In the same moment the claw caught on the pocket of her jacket, and as Milaroth tried to pull her back, the stitching tore and with another scream the girl launched herself forward into thin air.

Archer watched her arc outward, her arms and legs pinwheeling madly. She met the surface of the water with an explosive crash and vanished almost immediately.

Instinctively Archer went straight after her, all sound ceasing abruptly as water filled his ears.

Three meters down he held station, looking around for the girl.

The water was darker than a sealed coffin. He forced his pupils to expand but still it remained all but impenetrable.

He kicked for the surface, broke it and shook the water from his eyes.

There was still no sign of the girl.

Another growl made him twist around. Milaroth was gripping the railing, the metal twisting and wrenching out of shape as he flexed his claws impotently.

Archer looked back at him, knowing he was safe where he was. Land-based demons all shared an inbred hatred of the water, and this one was no exception.

That said, he felt safe in ignoring the demon, at least for the moment. A series of powerful strokes took him to the spot where the girl had entered the water. He dove again, all too aware of the time this was taking, that if he didn't find her soon she would drown for sure.

Around him the water swirled lazily like black blood. He searched quickly, but still found no sign of her.

Then —

As he broke surface again he saw her about ten or fifteen meters away, barely managing to hold her head above water. She was panicking, splashing, making a desperate, mewling, choking sound as she tried to keep from sinking again.

He quickly swam to her, pulled her to him, supported her. At first she flinched at his touch and when she looked at him her eyes were large and fear-blind in her near-bloodless, water-beaded face.

'*Tout va bien*,' he said.

Still watching them from the embankment, Milaroth roared his frustration.

Reaching a decision, Archer pulled the girl more firmly to him and then struck out one-handed for the far bank, which lay about two hundred meters away.

The girl was shivering violently. She was trying to speak but the words couldn't make it past her chattering teeth. Archer just kept swimming, seemingly tireless. Slowly the far bank came closer.

At last they slipped into the shadows between two moored cruisers and Archer boosted the girl up onto the wooden jetty there. He followed her up and got her to her feet.

Exhausted beyond belief, she studied him vaguely but with obvious suspicion. He wasn't even out of breath following the swim — though he certainly looked somewhat battered. He returned her gaze, watching as she tried to figure out who he was, who he could possibly be.

Then she swayed dangerously and he caught her before she could fall. She was weak and close to hypothermia — which made it vital that he keep her alert and moving.

'Wh-who . . . who are y-you?' she managed as they climbed a flight of mossy stone steps toward a point where the Promenade d'Australie joined Quai Branly. 'Wh-what *was* th-that thing?'

'Shhh,' he said, checking their surroundings and finding traffic on the broad thoroughfare to be virtually nonexistent. 'We'll talk in a while. But first we need to get you somewhere warm and dry.'

Instinctively she balked. Who was he, this man? How had he come to be mixed up in this . . . this . . . *whatever* it was?

Answers refused to come. But in the end she knew for sure that he had saved her life; that the same thing that had tried to kill him had tried to kill her, which made it a common enemy . . . and so she decided she could probably trust him.

He said, 'My hotel is — '

She silenced him with a shake of the head. 'M-my flat is cl-closer.'

He nodded, and allowed her to lead him along Quai Branley, back in the general direction of the clinic. The girl constantly kept looking back over one shoulder, but there was no sign of pursuit.

Gradually her dazed senses began to recover, though she continued to shiver almost uncontrollably. As they turned onto Rue de l'Université it started raining harder, and thunder knocked hollowly through the sky. The narrow street soon shone like patent leather.

About halfway along the thoroughfare she let him through a glass security door and into a narrow block of flats. Archer followed her up a dimly-lit staircase. Televisions pumped barely-heard music and chatter from various apartments.

When they reached the second floor he waited as she forced her stiff fingers to locate the key in the pocket of her jeans and unlock a black, windowless front door.

They went through into a narrow hallway. The first thing she did was turn on all the lights and close all the curtains. The flat, he noted, was small and functional. There was a small living room, an even smaller kitchen, a combination shower room and toilet and a single bedroom.

Without a word she vanished into the bedroom, closed the door and locked it behind her. Archer went into the living room, spotted a gas fire and, knowing the girl would need warmth, switched it on.

He thought about his attempt to slay Milaroth and how badly it had gone. Not only had the demon taken him by surprise, he had moved with a speed and power Archer had not expected, and it had thrown him completely.

Face it, he thought, *you're really not cut out for this.*

He winced suddenly and finally thought to check himself over. His jaw was slightly swollen and tender to the touch. His ribs and spine were aching and his muscles were starting to cramp and stiffen.

The bedroom door opened and the girl came out wearing old jogging pants and a matching sweat shirt, her wet hair still plastered to her head. She looked at him for a moment, then silently handed him a towel and a bathrobe. He took them and she turned and went lifelessly into the kitchen.

He quickly stripped off. He was lean and compact, with not an ounce of fat on him. But a series of large, angry-looking plum-colored bruises and scrapes bore testament to his recent encounter with Milaroth.

Ignoring them, he toweled himself dry, dumped his clothes in front of the fire, where they began to steam, and then slipped into the bathrobe. It was pink and fluffy and he felt ridiculous.

A minute or so later there was a discreet knock at the living room door.

'Come in,' he said.

She came in carrying two cups of hot chocolate. She gave him one and looked at him over the rim of her own. After a time she asked in a small voice, 'What was that thing?'

He wasn't used to girls, and this one fascinated him. Everything about her was petite, he thought. She was small and wiry, with fine, even features that would have looked pleasant were she not still so frightened.

He looked back at her and said, 'It's a demon.'

She accepted that with little more than a lowering of her eyelids, too exhausted to react any other way. 'And what are you?' she asked.

He wanted to tell her he was no-one special, just a passer-by, but his upbringing made him stick with the truth. 'I'm a demon-*slayer*,' he said.

'You didn't do very well tonight,' she noted.

He looked away from her, still ashamed by his failure. Then: 'Look . . . just . . . just forget what happened tonight.'

'I — '

'I know I'm asking the impossible,' he cut in. 'But trust me, you're better off not getting involved.'

'I'm *already* involved,' she reminded him irritably. 'That thing just tried to *kill* me! How easy do you think it will be to forget *that?*'

He looked away from her, feeling that sense of naïveté again, of being a stranger in a strange land where interaction with its inhabitants was something far, far beyond him.

Without warning, the phone on the small, circular coffee table between them began to ring. The girl flinched at the sound.

'Aren't you going to answer it?' asked Archer, when she made no move to do so.

She shook her head. 'I'm not in the mood for light conversation tonight.'

'It might be important.'

She glanced down at the caller ID. 'It is only Thierry.'

'Thierry?'

Abruptly, the phone stopped ringing. The silence was suddenly absolute.

'My name's Archer,' he said finally, to break it. 'What's yours?'

She sank gratefully into a chair, holding the cup in both hands, feeding off its warmth. 'Danielle Prevot,' she said. 'I work at the clinic. I'm a nurse there.' She looked at him carefully for a moment, then said, 'I saw it, that *thing*. Three nights ago. The night it killed those babies.'

'Go on,' he said.

She shrugged restively, clearly unnerved by the memory. 'I was just walking towards the clinic to start my shift when I saw . . . I don't know, *something* . . . it was like a shadow . . . it looked like it was sliding down the wall. At first I thought it was just a trick of the light, or my imagination. But then I saw that it had arms and legs . . . and a tail. Then it reached the ground and was gone.'

She shrugged again. 'I didn't really think any more about it. I just thought there was probably a natural explanation for it, or maybe I needed glasses . . . I went into work and was just hanging my coat up when I heard a disturbance in the maternity unit. You know what they found, of course?'

'Yes,' he said. 'And so you decided Milaroth was responsible.'

Her dark brows pinched together. 'Milaroth?'

'That's his name,' said Archer. 'Did you tell anyone what you saw?'

'No,' she said. 'In the first place I didn't have a clue what it was and in the second

I had no intention of saying anything about it in case my co-workers thought I was mad. These are hard times, *m'sieur*, I'm lucky just to have a job, and I certainly don't want to risk losing it. But . . .

'I cannot forget what I saw. And I have watched the clinic every night since it happened, because I wanted this . . . this thing to come back, to let me see it again. I was going to try to photograph it with my cell phone — which is now somewhere at the bottom of the Seine — and get some proof to back up what I saw. Instead I saw *you*, and you were acting so suspiciously that I decided to follow you, in case you could lead me to . . . him. *It*.'

'Well,' said Archer, 'now you know he's real.'

'Yes. And thank God, I have you to corroborate my story.'

'No you don't,' said Archer.

'You won't do it?'

'No,' he said.

'Why not?'

'Because there are some things your people are better off not knowing.'

'What do you mean, *'your people'*?' she snapped. 'You talk as if you're somehow different from the rest of us.'

Archer considered that. 'I am,' he said after a moment. 'And yet I'm not. It's complicated.'

'But if you tell the authorities whatever it is you know, they'll *have* to investigate!' she argued. 'They'll go back to that sewer and search until they find him.'

'He won't stay there now,' Archer said grimly. 'He'll find a new nest, a safer one.'

'And kill more babies?'

'Until he's stopped, yes.'

She stared moodily into the steam rising from her mug. 'Why does he kill these poor children, anyway?' she asked at last.

'They're a source of energy to him,' Archer replied, his mind elsewhere. 'He feeds off their very essence.'

She paled visibly, and when she spoke again there was a new tremble in her tone. 'Wh . . . what do you mean, he f-feeds off them?'

'I don't pretend to understand it any more than you do,' he confessed. 'All I

70

know is that he somehow takes from his victims all the things he himself can never possess. The spirit, the heart, the soul, the very *purity* of a newborn . . . everything it is and everything it will ever be, and by some process I can't even guess at, he's able to turn those essences into . . . nourishment.'

'And he . . . he *touched* me,' she whispered.

He realized suddenly that she'd started crying.

'I'm sorry,' he said. And stupidly: 'I didn't mean to upset you.'

She sniffed, then shook her head as if angry with herself. 'And you think you'll find him again?' she asked.

Archer hesitated, then said, '*Someone* will.'

She frowned. 'But not you?'

'No. Not me.'

'Why not? You fought him once. You had the courage to do that.'

'I'm not up to the task,' he said. 'I know that now.'

'But — '

Before she could say more, the doorbell

rang. Danielle stared at him, her eyes still haunted.

'Are you expecting anyone?' Archer asked tightly.

She shook her head.

The doorbell rang again. And then a voice outside said, 'I know you're in there, Champ, so quit clownin' around and open the goddam door.'

Archer recognized Palden's voice immediately.

6

As Palden pushed past him and into the living room, Archer said, 'How did you know where to find me?'

'I *always* know where to find you, Archer,' Palden replied irritably. 'By the way — pink really suits you.'

Archer stiffened self-consciously and immediately went over to the fire. He quickly pulled on his now as-near-as-dry jeans and shrugged out of the fluffy bathrobe.

'So,' said Palden. 'Did you *slay* him, like you *said* you would? Did it all go according to your wonderful *plan?*'

'You know it didn't,' snapped Archer, slipping into his T-shirt and then sitting down to lace up his still-steaming sneakers.

'Oh, I know it, all right,' said Palden. 'Because the goddam thing's standin' outside right now, waitin' for round *two!*'

'*What?*'

At last Danielle found her voice. 'Who is this man?' she asked Archer. Then, looking up into Palden's wide, golden-brown face, 'Who are you?'

'He's with me,' said Archer.

Palden shook his head. 'Uh-uh. *You're* with *me*, Champ, and don't you forget it.' He looked at Danielle. 'And you are . . . ?'

Archer quickly told him how Danielle fitted into it, then said, 'What do you mean, he's waiting outside?'

'He followed you here,' said Palden.

'How?'

Palden hooked a thumb over one shoulder. 'That your jacket hanging up outside, Cupcake?' he asked.

Danielle nodded. 'Of course.'

'What happened to the pocket?'

'That . . . that thing tried to grab me. He tore my pocket instead.'

'Then that's how he found you,' said Palden. 'By your scent.'

Her expression slackened. 'Like a dog, you mean?'

'More or less.'

'What are we going to do?' asked Archer.

Palden raised his eyebrows. 'Why ask *me?* This is your show, Champ. It's what's known as on-the-job training.'

Swallowing his pride, Archer said quietly, 'So train me.'

Palden looked at him, lifting one brow.

Archer said, grudgingly, '*Please.*'

Palden gave him a toothy grin. 'That's more like it. Okay, kids. First thing we gotta do is get out of here. If we have to fight, it's best we do it where we got plenty of room to maneuver and hardly any chance of injurin' anyone else caught in the crossfire. You got a car, Cupcake?'

Danielle shook her head.

'Okay, we'll steal one,' Palden decided at once. 'Sorry, *mam'selle*, but you'll have to come with us.'

She immediately backed away from him. 'Why?'

'Because if you don't, Milaroth's gonna come up here and grab you and use you as a hostage to put us right where he wants us. I'm not about to give him that chance.'

Archer said gently, 'He's right, Danielle. You'll be safer with us.'

She looked at Archer, trying to gauge just how far she could trust him. Finally she nodded and went past them to get another jacket.

Palden said, 'Harder than it looks, isn't it? Being a Demon-Slayer?'

Archer nodded. '*Too* hard.'

Five minutes later they left the flat and took the stairs down to the ground floor. Around them, the muted television-sounds confirmed that the other tenants were blissfully unaware of the drama unfolding literally on their doorstep.

Archer went to the glass front door and peered out. It was still raining, the downpour stitching puddles and making the overworked drains gurgle. The street looked empty.

Palden joined him, moving as silently as thought. After a moment the tall black man muttered, '*Shoot.*'

'What?'

'Can't you *feel* it, Champ?'

Archer scanned the street again. It looked as empty as before, but this time something indefinable sent a shiver down his spine.

76

'There are *two* of them out there,' he whispered.

Palden nodded. 'Yeah. Looks like Milaroth's fetched a playmate with him.' He wheeled around, said, 'Is there a back way out of here, Cupcake?'

'There is a yard that opens onto the next street over,' said Danielle.

'All right,' said Palden. 'I'm gonna go get us some wheels. Stay right here, an' come runnin' the minute I pull up outside.'

Archer grabbed him by the arm. 'Wait a minute. Why don't we all just go out the back way?'

Palden rolled his eyes. 'Come *on*, Champ, keep up,' he muttered irritably. 'We *want* those demons to follow us 'cause we need to get 'em away from all the good folks that live around here.'

Without waiting for a response, the black man vanished along the passage beside the staircase.

After he'd gone, Danielle came to stand beside Archer. He felt her arm slide softly through his and her touch sent a shock through him, which reminded him about what Palden had said earlier about the pleasure of bumping fuzzies.

His curiosity on that score, however, would have to wait.

'I can't believe this is really happening,' Danielle said miserably.

'Neither can I,' he replied. 'I never thought . . . '

'What?'

'Nothing.'

'No, go on.'

'I never thought it was going to be like this. Ever. I thought it was all going to be so straightforward.'

'Nothing is *ever* straightforward,' she whispered, and her tone was suddenly, curiously dead. 'I can see that now.'

A few minutes passed, tortuously slow. Then they heard a distant squeal of tires and Danielle stiffened.

'Get ready,' said Archer.

A few seconds later a silver Fiat 500 fishtailed to an untidy halt in front of the apartment block and the passenger side door sprang open.

Archer yelled, *'Go!'*

He tore the front door open and shoved

Danielle ahead of him. At once they were pounded by rain. The girl splashed toward the car just as Palden, behind the wheel, the guts of the ignition system trailing from the dashboard onto his lap like multicolored spaghetti, pulled the passenger seat forward and urgently waved her in.

She threw herself forward and more or less dove onto the small back seat. In the same moment, Milaroth broke cover from a tall doorway forty meters away and came crashing through the storm, water starbursting up beneath his feet.

Archer got halfway to the car, then froze.

Palden yelled, '*Champ!*'

Ignoring him, Archer twisted toward the oncoming demon, raised both hands and cried, '*Fire, Earth, Water, Wind, lend me your power, lend me your strength, come to me when I call your names . . . So Mote It Be!*'

Nothing.

Deep inside him a little voice said, *Told you you weren't cut out for this.*

But again he set himself and bawled, *'Fire, Earth, Water, Wind, lend me your power, lend me your strength, come to me when I call your names . . . SO MOTE IT BE!'*

It seemed to Danielle, watching from the back seat, that a single bar of semi-translucent light suddenly burst silently from each of Archer's palms. They shot toward Milaroth, each of them about as thick around as a can of soda-pop, and when they struck the demon he pulled up sharp, as if he'd just run into an invisible barrier.

The force of the beams knocked him backwards; he spilled against a car but came up again almost at once.

Incredibly, Archer actually went forward to meet him. *'Fire and thunder rise together and banish this evil for all the harm it has done!'*

Again some kind of beam shot from Archer's hands, and it lit up the rain around it as it surged forward and smashed Milaroth in the face.

The demon jerked, howled and, weakened, dropped to one knee. The ground seemed to shake beneath them as he went down.

'*Quit showboatin'!*' bawled Palden.

Much as Archer wanted to finish Milaroth while he still could, he knew Palden was right; it *was* too heavily populated here for such combat.

Reluctantly he threw himself into the Fiat and Palden floored the accelerator even before he had the door shut.

The car leapt forward with a screech of burning rubber. In the rear-view mirror Archer saw Milaroth push back to his feet, drop to all fours and start loping after them like some monstrous, spike-spined dog.

Up ahead a second demon had planted itself directly in their path.

Archer's eyes widened as they sped toward it. The thing was big and heavy, its stocky body encircled by band upon band of cable-thick muscles beneath skin that was the color of dry red clay. It had a small, horned head that seemed to rise straight out of the upward slope of its massive shoulders, a deep chest, a chunky waist and thick, muscular legs.

In the merest sliver of a second Archer identified the demon exactly as he had been trained to do.

It was Ye'terel, brother of Milaroth: a minor earth demon, still relatively young by the standards of his species, traditionally responsible for blight and famine, the poisoning of rivers and wells back in Tibet, the indiscriminate killing of yaks, *dris*, sheep and goats, and a general bringer of hardship.

'What you got up your sleeve now, Champ?' Palden asked tightly.

Archer thought fast. 'Charm of the Beast Spell?'

'No time,' said Palden. 'Cupcake?'

'*O-Oui, m'sieur?*'

'Hang on!'

Palden kept the Fiat aimed at the demon until the last possible moment, then yanked hard on the wheel. The little car turned, rising up onto its two offside tires, and shot through a gap between parked cars and onto the pavement.

Ye'terel twisted at the waist and spat some kind of guttural oath. His breath fogged the car's windows as it sped past.

Then Palden twisted the wheel again and they crashed back into the narrow road —

— and came to a whiplash-inducing dead stop.

Archer twisted at the waist and saw that Ye'terel had grabbed the Fiat by its rear bumper and was lifting it off the ground so that its occupants began to tip forward, Palden and Archer toward the dashboard, Danielle thumping against the back of Palden's seat with a screech.

* * *

'*Non ... non ... s'il vous plait à Dieu —* '

Ye'terel started to shake the car, snarling as he did so.

Archer's eyes dropped to the side mirror, where he could see Milaroth still charging up the street toward them, moving faster than a rhino. '*Palden! Get us out of here!*'

Before Palden could bite off a reply there was a sudden wrenching scream from the back of the car and Ye'terel staggered backward, holding the twisted rear bumper in his claws.

At the same moment the Fiat bounced back onto the ground and Palden floored the accelerator. The little car shot forward with a squeal, slipping and sliding until the black man finally regained control.

'*God bless lousy French workmanship!*' he roared.

'Fiat is Italian,' Danielle corrected him quickly.

'French, Italian, what's the difference? If the damn' piece of junk hadn't fallen apart when it did we'd be chopped beef by now!'

Ye'terel hurled the bumper after them, using it like a spear. It missed the car, hit the tarmac and skittered across to the far sidewalk in a shower of sparks.

Archer's eyes shuttled up to the rearview mirror. Milaroth was still charging after them, and now Ye'terel was stamping along in his wake, the pair of them still determined to catch their prey.

'Can . . . can we outrace them?' asked Danielle, her voice diminutive in the shadows of the back seat.

'That,' said Palden, not bothering to turn around, 'is a very good question, Cupcake.'

7

They roared out onto Avenue du
Maréchal Gallieni with the window
wipers struggling to keep the rain-
spattered windscreen clear. Palden
wrenched on the wheel and sent them
skidding to the right in a great silver
spray of standing water, onto a wide and
mercifully almost deserted road.

As they crossed the Voie Express Rive
Gauche, a car coming at them from the
left braked hard to avoid a collision.
There was the angry blaring of a horn,
and then the car spun out toward the
sidewalk, where it rocked on its
suspension like a wet dog shaking itself
dry.

Palden paid the vehicle no attention,
just kept them blurring right across Pont
Alexandre.

'They still with us, Cupcake?' he called
over one shoulder.

Danielle turned back from the rear

window. 'I think they're gaining on us!' she reported fearfully. 'The red one definitely is.'

The Fiat came off the bridge and again made a right on two squealing wheels. The car fishtailed madly as it sped on along the tree-lined Voie Georges Pompidou. The road narrowed down to two lanes, separated by an avenue of bare, storm-lashed trees that ran along its center.

As Port de la Concorde came up on their right the Fiat made a sickening lurch and dropped toward an underpass. All at once the little car was filled with quick-strobing amber light.

Danielle said, 'Oh God, that thing is definitely gaining on us, that red thing!'

Archer ducked his head a little so that he could check the side mirror again. 'She's right,' he told Palden.

The car shot up out of the underpass. Danielle felt as if she'd left her stomach behind and managed, 'I . . . th-think I'm going to be sick.'

'Oh, *puh-lease* . . . ' muttered Palden.

'Leave her be,' snapped Archer.

'All right,' said Palden. 'We need a

87

miracle right about now, Champ. What do you suggest?'

Archer glanced at the black man's profile and decided he was just about the most irritating person he was ever likely to meet. 'I don't know.'

'Champ, that is *not* the kind of answer we want to hear right now.'

'Then *you* come up with something!' yelled Archer. 'All I've done so far is make everything worse!'

'You want me to do somethin'?' Palden demanded. 'Is that it?'

'Yes!'

'You *sure* about that, Champ?'

'I said so, didn't I?'

'All right. See how you like *this*.'

With a shrug Palden stamped on the brake and the Fiat suddenly howled to a stop, leaving a wake of rubber smoking against the greasy asphalt.

Danielle threw herself against the back of Palden's seat, her nausea temporarily forgotten. 'What are you doing? It'll catch up!'

Ignoring her, Palden twisted in his seat and glared hard at Archer. 'Now, you listen up, Champ, an' you listen *good!*' he grated. 'Just in case it happened to slip your mind for a second, you're a Demon-Slayer, *capice?* You've spent the last twenty-one years learnin' how to *slay* these jokers — so why don't you just go out there an' do your damn' job?'

Archer stared at him. 'Tell me how!' he demanded stubbornly.

Palden rolled his eyes again. 'Champ, I ain't got time to draw you a diagram — '

'I'm only asking for guidance!'

'Remember what I said about on-the-job training?'

Cursing his unkind fate, Archer shouldered the door open and stepped out into the storm. Ye'terel was no more than a hundred meters away now — just about as close as Archer, now beside himself with fury, was prepared to let him get.

He went back to meet the onrushing demon and then planted himself in the middle of the crossroads so that his reflection grew straight down from the soles of his sneakers into the soaking road. Raising his voice he called, '*Air!*'

He moved one hand from his top left to

his top right to accompany the cry.

'*Fire!*'

Again a motion with his hand, this one moving from his bottom right to middle corner.

'*Water!*'

Top right to top left corner.

'*Earth!*'

Bottom left to top middle corner.

Watching from the car, Palden narrowed his eyes and murmured almost grudgingly, 'Lesser Ritual of the Pentagram. Good call.'

'*Ateh!*' Archer intoned. '*Malkuth! Ve-Gedulah! Le-Olahm! Yahd-Hey-Vau-Hey!*'

Ye'terel slowed to a trot and his tiny round head seemed to sink into his shoulders. His mouth opened impossibly wide and as he screamed his defiance at the spell, worms fell from where they had been lodged between his teeth to land on the wet roadway, there to wriggle and contort this way and that.

Archer strode forward, moving quickly now, with obvious purpose, his every sense focused fairly and squarely on the red giant who now came to a halt before him.

'Adoni!' he called, using one finger to trace first a semi-circle, then a pentagram. 'Ehyeh!' Again the pentagram. 'Atah Gibor Le-Olamh Adonai!'

He extended his hand and made a sign very much like a cross.

'Before Me, Raphael! Behind me, Gabriel! At my right hand, Mee-Chye-Ehl! At my left hand, Uriel!'

Ye'terel reared back, but seemed unable to move from the spot. He turned and looked back over one sloping shoulder. Milaroth was still down on all fours and loping ever closer, but he had never been as fleet as his young brother and Ye'terel knew he would never get here in time to prevent the inevitable conclusion to the ritual.

He twisted back to face Archer, snarled, bunched his massive red hands into fists and then began to stalk forward.

Standing his ground, Archer yelled, 'About me flames the pentagram, and in the column shines the six-rayed star!'

No sooner had the last word left his lips

than he stamped his right foot and —

In the car, Danielle whispered, *'Mon Dieu . . . '*

At first she thought they were snakes — two strange, golden snakes whipping and slipping across the ground between Archer and the demon he had set out to slay. It was only when they slid up over the flailing demon and wrapped themselves around him, one crossing from Ye'terel's left shoulder to his right hip, the other crossing itself from his right shoulder to his left hip, that she realized they were in fact . . . *chains*.

Again Archer called, *'Air!'* and moved one hand from his top left to his top right. *'Fire!'* Bottom right to middle corner. *'Water!'* Top right to top left corner. *'Earth!'* Bottom left to top middle corner.

Ye'terel's crimson eyes swelled to the size of saucers.

'Ateh!' Archer intoned. *'Malkuth! Ve-Gedulah! Le-Olahm! Yahd-Hey-Vau-Hey!'*

And then it happened.

As if invisible hands had taken hold of them, the chains began to tighten themselves around Ye'terel's torso, tighten, *tighten* . . .

Danielle watched as they bit ever deeper into Ye'terel's spongy flesh, as blood that looked more like sludge oozed from the splits, as Ye'terel raised his face to the lightning-lit night and howled his anguish.

But the chains grew tighter still, and began to sink slowly, inexorably into the cuts they were deepening with every passing second.

And then —

And then —

All at once the chains grew so tight that Ye'terel gave one final bellow and just —

— *exploded.*

There was a sudden crash of sound like thunder that wasn't thunder at all, and then Ye'terel vanished in a thick crimson spray.

When it cleared all that was left of the demon was a pile of raw, steaming chunks of meat from which the golden chains slowly began to fade.

Further back down the road Milaroth thumped to a halt, having witnessed the ritual and its outcome. He pushed up onto his feet and when he howled the sound held fury and loss in equal measure.

Palden called, 'Okay, Champ! Get back in the car!'

Archer shook his head, clearly pumped up. 'No! I can finish this, right here and now!'

'The hell you can! You might've chosen one of the Lesser Rituals, but it's still gonna leave you drained!'

Milaroth broke into a sprint, coming closer. Archer watched him come, ripped between wanting to show what he could do and wanting to run, all the while knowing that Palden was right.

He threw himself back into the car before his now-shaky legs could give way altogether.

Palden got them moving again. Archer watched Milaroth come to a halt beside all that remained of Ye'terel and once again howl at the raging sky.

'Where are we going?' he asked.

His voice had a curious choked quality to it.

Palden didn't bother to answer. He made a slight left onto Quai de la Mégisserie, then another onto Quai de Louvre. Gradually the large, official-looking buildings to either side gave way to smaller shops, all sensibly shut at this time of night.

Another bridge took them back across the river, after which Palden followed a sharp left with an equally sharp right, onto the deserted Rue de la Cité.

A few minutes later they reached their destination — the holiest site in Paris.

Notre Dame Cathedral.

★　★　★

Notre Dame sits on the eastern side of the Île de la Cité, one of only two natural islands in the Seine, and it is a site the cathedral has occupied for almost a millennium. The official chair of the Archbishop of Paris, and said to hold the original Crown of Thorns worn by Christ, no demon would dare venture anywhere near it.

As the storm continued to play itself

out, the building loomed over them, grand and intricate in its fussy Gothic architecture, some interior light making its rose windows glow comfortingly through the squally darkness.

Palden killed the engine and they sat there for a while, listening to the irregular tick it made cooling down, and the rain drumming impatiently at the roof.

'We'll be safe enough here till dawn,' he told Danielle at last. 'Ain't a demon been spawned who'd risk settin' foot anywhere near *this* place.'

She nodded vaguely, then asked, 'Why until dawn?'

'Demons are nocturnal, most of 'em,' he explained. 'Milaroth'll find himself a bolt-hole long before the sun comes up.'

'But he'll be back again tomorrow night? To . . . to kill more babies?'

'Oh, sure. And that's when we'll finish him once and for all; right, Champ?'

Archer twisted in his seat and shook his head. 'That's when *you'll* finish him,' he said. 'I just quit.'

'*What?*'

'You heard me. I was taught to slay

demons. All right — I just slew one. Now I'm out of here.'

'Sure, you slew *a* demon,' allowed Palden. 'But you didn't slay *the* demon.'

'I don't care. I've got other things I want to do with my life.'

'Your life's already been mapped out for you, Champ.'

'Not by me it hasn't,' Archer retorted. 'The Ancients kidnapped me, Palden — '

'Ah, here we go again.'

' — they stole me away from my family, just like they stole you away from yours. If you're willing to stand for that, that's up to you. But I'm different.'

'Oh, really? Do tell.'

'Forget it, you wouldn't understand.'

'I might understand better than you know, Champ.'

'I doubt it.'

Danielle said, 'Archer! You can't just walk away from this!'

He threw her a look. 'You don't know anything about it. Anything about *me*.'

'But I know what I saw,' she shot back. 'A thing that killed twelve innocent babies before they could even *begin* to live. A

97

thing that needs to pay for that!'

'I'm not saying he shouldn't. But why should it be me who slays him?'

'Because you're this . . . this Demon-Slayer,' she said.

'So is he,' Archer replied, gesturing toward Palden.

'Yeah, I am,' Palden admitted. 'But you're *fresh*, Champ. That's the difference. After forty-odd years in this cockeyed business, I'm just about spent. The best I can probably manage is to *contain* Milaroth, the way Tilonus did. *If* I'm lucky.'

'So get lucky and contain him,' snapped Archer. 'And then tell the Ancients to send you another Slayer.'

Palden reached for his cigarettes. 'All right, Champ — *walk*. I'm damned if I'm gonna beg you to stay.'

'Oh, I'm going, don't worry. And before you get the wrong idea, it's not because I'm scared.'

''Course it's not.'

'*It's not!*'

'Methinks the Slayer doth protest too much,' paraphrased Palden. He was about to light a cigarette when Danielle touched him on the shoulder and shook her head.

'I'd sooner you didn't,' she said.

'Well, think what you like,' Archer said irritably as Palden stuffed the cigarette back into the pack. 'But I'll tell you now, my mind's been made up about this since I was eight years old. And you're not going to stop me.'

'*I* don't *have* to,' Palden said softly.

'What does *that* mean?'

'You'll find out.' And then he turned to study Archer and said bluntly, 'Are you still here?'

Angrily Archer reached for the door lock. 'Not anymore.'

He got out of the Fiat, slammed the door behind him and stamped off through the storm. Palden watched him go, the window wipers still squeaking back and forth, back and forth.

Slowly, thoughtfully, he tucked the cigarette packet back into his jacket pocket.

'What are we going to do now?' asked Danielle.

He craned his neck to look back at her.

'I'll take you back to your flat at dawn,' he replied. 'You should be safe enough from now on, but I'll surround you with a couple of protection spells just to make sure.'

'I mean about Milaroth,' she pressed.

He shook his head. 'I got me some serious thinkin' to do on that score,' he muttered. 'If I'm gonna kill 'em all.'

She tilted her head at him. '*Them?* What do you mean, *them?* There's only the one demon . . . isn't there?'

'There are three,' he replied. 'Milaroth had three brothers; Ye'terel, Amorion and Skarasis. Archer just killed Ye'terel. Now Milaroth's gonna summon the other two, and together they're gonna make this city pay.'

'Can you possibly beat them?' she whispered.

'One way to find out,' he said grimly.

She shook her head in frustration as she watched Archer vanish into the night, shoulders hunched, head down. 'What's his problem, anyway?' she demanded impatiently.

Palden hesitated briefly. Then he

seemed to sag a little, as if the weight of years had finally caught up with him, and all at once he didn't look fashionable and streetwise anymore, he just looked old and tired. As if suddenly feeling the need to unburden himself, he said softly, 'Come up here beside me, Cupcake, and I'll tell you.'

8

Dawn over Paris.

The new day began bright and calm. The sun shone from a cloudless blue sky, it was noticeably warmer than it had been for weeks, and the sweet promise of spring made itself felt throughout the city.

Archer came awake with a start and looked around his hotel room. He half-expected to see Palden sitting in one of the armchairs, cigarette in hand, watching him with that faintly mocking expression of his. But he was all alone.

Good.

Still, he was uncomfortably aware that things had not really gone according to plan. Ever since he was a boy, he had rehearsed this moment time and again in his mind. The Ancients would finally send him out into the world on some mission or other and he would simply vanish at the first opportunity, only to show up again some unspecified time later in

America where, under a new identity, he would begin his search for his long-lost family.

Instead, he'd met Palden and come to realize that he wasn't quite as free as he'd expected to be. He'd fought two demons and killed one, and it had been dirty, unpleasant, dangerous work that he did not feel at all cut out for.

And when he'd looked into Danielle Prevot's eyes he'd felt his first real stirring of emotion for another human being. It wasn't love — even *he* wasn't naïve enough to believe that — but it was some kind of spiritual connection that was new to him, new and curiously . . . *right*.

He didn't want to feel that he was letting her down. He *wasn't*. Palden would deal with Milaroth. He'd slay or banish the Feaster and that would be an end to it.

Wouldn't it?

He hated the guilt that suddenly assailed him and in a foul mood he showered, dressed and then stared out over the waking city. Whatever happened here today, or tomorrow, or the day after

. . . it was no longer any business of his.

But it was you who killed Ye 'terel, his conscience reminded him. *Whatever Milaroth does now will be a direct consequence of that.*

Deciding that he needed distraction, he went down to the restaurant and ordered a bowl of bland, unsweetened oatmeal. Still deep in thought, he ate without tasting a single mouthful.

Not for the first time, he wondered if every Demon-Slayer felt the same temptation to turn his back on the life Fate had ordained for him. Had some of them at least ever succumbed to it? And if they had, had they regretted it? Or were they out there somewhere even now, living normal lives, with wives and children and regular jobs, memories of the Red Cap Monastery already dimmed if not entirely forgotten?

He had no answers.

Afterwards, back in the privacy of his room, he got the number for Air France and used the credit card he'd been given to book a one-way ticket to Washington, D.C. Since he had no real idea yet where his search would take him, he figured he might just as well begin in the nation's capital.

He was just finishing the call when there was a knock at the door. He hung up and went to answer it, believing he already knew the identity of his visitor.

As he opened the door he said, 'I hope you've come to say goodbye, Palden, because — '

His voice died in his throat.

'Can I come in?' asked Danielle Prevot.

Just the sight of her did something electric to him that he was unable to understand. But then his dark mood came crashing back to replace it. Recovering from his surprise and trying not to show her just how pleased he was to see her, he muttered stubbornly, 'Not if Palden put you up to coming here.'

'He didn't.'

'But he must have told you where to find me.'

'I asked him,' she explained testily. 'But I don't think he knew I intended to actually come and see you. I mean, what would be the point?'

'Exactly,' he replied.

He remained where he was for a moment, torn between telling her to leave and letting her in. But since she looked so forlorn, there was no way he could do the former.

As he closed the door behind her he said, 'Well, we might as well get one thing straight from the outset. There's nothing you can do or say to make me change my mind about this.'

'I know,' she replied, her tone still frosty. 'That's why I want you to tell *me* how to slay Milaroth.'

He snorted. 'Are you crazy?'

'Tell me what to do, what to say, and *I'll* do it,' she said with absolute determination.

She walked deeper into the room and loosened the belt of her charcoal gray woolen coat. Beneath it she wore a print blouse tucked into a pair of satin suit trousers. She looked gorgeous, and again he knew a fleeting moment of curiosity about the bumping of fuzzies.

'You wouldn't last five seconds against Milaroth,' he told her softly.

'Nevertheless, someone must try.'

'Yes. *Palden*.'

'*I* will do it,' she said with absolute determination. 'If you will teach me.'

He shook his head. 'All I'd be doing is sending you to your death, and I won't do that.'

To his surprise her lip curled unpleasantly and she snapped bitterly, 'You think life holds any meaning for me now?'

He narrowed his eyes, puzzled by the statement. 'I don't — '

'No, you *don't*,' she interrupted, suddenly fidgety and fighting tears. 'You don't know *anything*, except what *you* want.'

'I — '

'I, I, I!' she mimicked. 'Don't you ever get tired of thinking about *yourself* all the time?'

'Is that why you came here?' he asked, his own temper flaring. 'To tell me what a bad person I am because all I want is the right to live my own life?'

'No. I came because I want to kill Milaroth.'

'And I told you, Palden will do that.'

'Palden doesn't have the strength. He isn't as fresh as you.'

'He'll manage.'

'And if he doesn't?' She glared up at him, the tears still glistening in her eyes. 'Do you want *his* death on your conscience as well?'

He was about to offer a retort but bit off suddenly. 'What do you mean, his death *as well*? I didn't kill those babies! I didn't even know anything about — '

'No,' she agreed. 'But . . . but . . . '

She heeled around and went over to the window, where she stared out at the city.

'I'm not talking about *those* babies, Archer,' she managed at last. 'I'm talking about *my* baby.'

'*What?*'

'Last week I took a test,' she said, her shoulders starting to hitch again. 'I'm *pregnant*, Archer . . . or rather, I *was* pregnant up until yesterday evening.'

She turned back to him, her face a portrait in despair. 'Now do you get it? Thierry and I were going to have a baby, and it was the most wonderful news we could have hoped for. But then I encountered your demon who kills babies for nourishment, and he *touched* me, Archer . . . he *touched* me! And because of that my baby is *also* dead.'

Without seeming to be aware of it, she rubbed her stomach gently. 'And so I will kill *him*,' she continued grimly. 'And for once you will stop thinking only of yourself and you will show me how.'

He stared at her for a long moment, his already turbulent emotions suddenly even more conflicted. As he groped for the right thing to say he felt genuine compassion for her, and yet there was something else in him too; a selfish regret that she already had a partner . . . that there was no way she would ever be his.

'You're wrong,' he murmured.

'You told me so yourself,' she replied. 'What he does . . . how he takes the very life-force of the young and somehow converts it into energy . . . *food*.'

He nodded. 'That's true. But he's known as the Feaster on Newborn-Souls, Danielle. *Newborn* souls. I don't know why, but until a baby is born, it's safe inside its mother.'

She stopped crying in mid-sob, stared at him, trying to decide if he was telling her the truth or just something that would calm her down.

'I promise you,' he said earnestly. And without waiting, he crossed the room, reached out and tried to take her hands away from her stomach.

Instinctively she resisted him. 'What are you doing?' she said.

'Trust me,' he told her.

He gently set his left palm against the slight swell of her belly, his expression intent, his eyes focused on something far, far away. All she could do was stand there, and watch, and wait.

A moment later his shoulders slumped and she knew that he had only succeeded in confirming what she already felt — that her baby was dead.

Then he smiled.

'You're baby's alive and well,' he said, and a crazy and entirely uncharacteristic chuckle escaped from him. 'She's strong and healthy, Danielle!'

She muttered, 'Sh . . . *she?*'

'She's fine,' he confirmed. 'I promise you.'

She started crying again, but with relief this time, and knowing he had to do something with her but not necessarily knowing what, he finally took her awkwardly in his arms and offered her a parental pat on the shoulder.

'There, there,' he said, feeling completely at a loss.

She hugged him in return and wept against his chest, all the fear and dread she had harbored since the night before suddenly banished. She smelled of mangos and pears, of jasmine, red hibiscus, sandalwood and lotus flowers, and though he tried not to he found the mixture intoxicating.

'You . . . you'd better call Thierry,' he said quietly. 'Tell him everything's okay.'

She pushed back from him and said, 'He doesn't even know there was a problem.'

'You didn't tell him?'

'What could I tell him that he would ever believe?'

He searched desperately for something

to say in reply, then realized suddenly that he was looking directly into her eyes and she was looking deeply, searchingly, back into his.

The room was silent.

He wondered then if she felt the same emotional connection that he did; whether that same connection was stronger with him than it was with her and Thierry, and if it was, whether or not she expected him to kiss her.

He knew suddenly that she did. Her eyelids dropped, her lips parted slightly and —

— and with a supreme effort of will he stepped back from her, let her go.

Flustering, seemingly as confused by her own emotions as he was by his, she sniffed, tugged a handkerchief from her jacket pocket and said, 'I still want you to tell me how to kill Milaroth.'

He let his breath go and finally released her. 'It can't be done. Not without a lifetime of training.'

'Then I'll just have to cram,' she said. 'He'll be back again after dark, you know.'

'I know,' he replied. 'Bad things *always*

happen at night. But it can't be done.'

'Then it falls to *you*,' she whispered.

Irritably, he turned away from her. 'I told you — my mind's made up. There's nothing you can say that'll change it.'

'I think there *is*,' she replied.

Again, something in her tone made him look back at her.

'You want to find your parents, your family,' she said. 'It's all you want.'

'More or less,' he agreed reluctantly.

'Because you have always felt that a part of you is missing,' she went on.

'How did you know that?'

'Palden told me everything, last night.'

'What does *he* know about it?'

'You might be surprised.'

'All right,' he muttered uneasily. 'Go on.'

'Well, you're right, Archer. But you're wrong, as well.'

'Look, I don't mean to sound rude, but I really don't have time for this. I've just booked my flight out of here. I'm leaving at eleven-fifteen tonight.'

'But I can *help* you,' she said urgently.

'How?'

'I can explain why you feel the way you do. Why you have *always* felt that way.'

'So explain it,' he said.

She looked at him for a long, uncomfortable moment. Then she said, 'There *is* a part of you that's missing, Archer. It's your twin sister.'

A tingle that was in no way pleasant tightened his skin. '*What?*'

'I don't pretend to understand it all,' she went on, 'but I understand *some* of it, I think. You're the seventh son of the seventh son of the seventh son, and because of that you were . . . I don't know — *abducted?* . . . by a group known as the Ancients, to fight another group known as the Council of Thirteen.'

'I already know that.'

'But did you know that this Council of Thirteen *also* scours the earth in search of these self-same seventh sons? So that they can . . . recruit . . . them for their own purposes?'

His unease began to grow. 'No.'

'The same night the Ancients snatched you away from your family, one of the Council's agents, or demons, or whatever you want to call them, also tried to abduct you. There was a struggle and the demon was injured and fled. You were stolen away and taken to Tibet, where you were raised and trained as a Demon-Slayer.

'But the very next night, that same demon returned and stole away your sister, reasoning that, since you both shared such a close biological tie, she might have powers or potential to match your own.'

Danielle looked wretched as she told him, 'Archer — she was taken to the Council of Thirteen and raised to combat you and all the other Demon-Slayers at work in the world.'

He swallowed audibly. 'How . . . how does Palden know all this?' he managed.

Again she hesitated. Then: 'He was the Slayer who stole you away that night.'

Archer felt numb, unable to fully comprehend what he was hearing. And yet he remembered something Narayan had said when he was eight years old.

We are all different, child. No two are ever exactly the same.

No two are ever exactly the same.

Danielle went on, 'Palden told me — and I believe him — that he has often been tempted to stop being a Slayer, to go his own way and make his own life, much as you plan to do now. But one thing has always stopped him. Your sister.'

'Why?'

'As Palden explained it to me, you never had any real choice in this. Fate had already decreed that you would be a Demon-Slayer. But your sister, she was an innocent party, and Palden believes he led the Council of Thirteen not only to you, but also unwittingly to *her*.'

'And that's why he stays?'

'He hopes one day to rescue her.'

Archer stared at her, trying to work out whether or not this was some elaborate mind game of Palden's to make him think twice before leaving. But when he looked into the girl's eyes all he could see there was sincerity. Besides, knowing that he had a twin sister out there somewhere wouldn't make him stay *here*, it would only make him more determined to strike out elsewhere, in search of her.

'What . . . ' he began. Then, 'What's her name?'

'Gadreel,' said the girl. 'That's the name the Council has given her.'

'Then *I'll* find her,' he said softly, 'and rescue her.'

He sounded determined. But at the back of his mind a tiny voice that would not be silenced said, *That's if it's not already too late.*

'Then you and Palden want the same thing,' she told him.

'He only wants it to ease his conscience.'

'Of course he does. But that still gives you a common purpose.'

'And for that, what?' he demanded. 'I'm supposed to go help him, now?'

'You heard him,' she said. 'He doesn't have the strength left to fight *one* demon, much less *three*.'

'Three?' he asked, surprised.

'Milaroth's brothers. They'll want to make you pay for slaying that thing, that . . . Ye'terel. And if they can't find you, Palden says they'll lay waste to the city in *your* name, to make sure you suffer the way they've suffered.'

Archer turned away from her, but almost against his will he asked, 'What does Palden have in mind?'

'I don't know,' she replied. 'But I know he's going to try to kill them all in one go, if he can — tonight.'

'Where?' he asked.

She gestured toward the window. 'There.'

He turned back again, followed her line of sight until his eyes came to rest . . . on the Eiffel Tower.

9

Père Lachaise Cemetery is the largest burial ground in Paris. Situated in the northeastern quarter of the city and named after Père Francois de la Chaise, Jesuit priest and *confidante* to Louis XIV, it is the final resting place for more than one million souls — three times that number if you include the remains that are stored within its ossuary, a bewildering network of catacombs off-limits to visitors.

Within the cemetery's high stone walls lies a virtual city, replete with tree-lined avenues and rolling hills, cobbled gutters and worn stone steps edged with moss. Affectionately known by Parisians as *Le Cité des Morts* — The City of the Dead — it is a necropolis in the truest sense of the word.

In all respects, Nicolas Bausang loved Père Lachaise. Who wouldn't love to work within such close proximity to the likes of

Chopin and Piaf, Oscar Wilde and Bizet?

Of course, Nicolas could have well done without Jim Morrison, as could almost every other member of staff. Oh, it was nothing personal, just that The Doors front-man attracted too many visitors of . . . well, the wrong sort . . . and their tributes of whiskey and cigarettes, plus their tendency to smoke pot and have sex right in front of the rock star's shrine, was simply not welcome here.

Nicolas had worked at Père Lachaise for four years. Of average height, a touch overweight and cursed with a five o'clock shadow that no amount of close or careful shaving could ever completely eradicate, he was a Grounds Maintenance Operative, which was an elaborate title for a fairly mundane job. Primarily he was a gardener, though sometimes he pitched in and helped dig graves or other such tasks when the need arose. In his time he had even assisted in more than a few exhumations.

But it was an occupation that suited the inoffensive, round-faced young man perfectly. He'd always been a loner. Even though he was now part of a workforce one hundred strong, he still kept mostly to himself. And the sober, tranquil nature of the cemetery, so different from the frenetic hustle and bustle of the Paris beyond its precincts, suited his retiring character quite literally down to the ground.

Unfortunately Nicolas took after his mother, who had always been a somewhat gloomy soul. She had never really come to terms with losing her elderly mother to cancer, or subsequently being abandoned by Nicolas's father, who had been unable to deal with her persistent melancholy. From these events she had concluded that life was, overall, a rather disappointing business, and this outlook she had communicated to her only son almost as soon as he was old enough to comprehend it.

Unsurprisingly, Nicolas himself had grown into a shy, withdrawn child. His formative years had been filled with so many terrible stories about how his mother had been forced to watch his grandmother die slowly and painfully and been powerless to stop it, that he had come to dread the day when his own mother — the only family he had — passed away.

In the end, however, her death when he was just sixteen had been a revelation to him, for in order to attend his mother's funeral he also had to make his first-ever visit to a cemetery . . . and it was there that he finally found the sense of peace and wellbeing that had always hitherto eluded him. From that moment on he viewed a graveyard — any graveyard — as a sanctuary from the outside world, a place where he could finally relax, soak up the stillness and simply be himself.

A string of office jobs had occupied his late teens and early twenties. Most of them had ended in his dismissal. He was by no means a bad worker, but he always found it difficult to fit in and become part of the team — and that was something his employers deemed vital to the performance of his duties.

So it was that he finally decided to find work in an altogether more conducive setting . . . and that was how he ended up at Père Lachaise. The work was physically demanding, but Nicolas was never happier than when he was lost among all the tombs and headstones, beautifying the surroundings he loved so much.

He never tired of this home of the dead. Indeed, it was a constant source of fascination to him. Elaborate chapels stood alongside cramped tombs and together they formed almost magical mazes of weathered stone, while the monuments themselves — he had once heard that there were seventy thousand of them, and he could well believe it — could range from the highly structured to the deceptively simple.

He was just pushing his wheelbarrow back through the autumn-dark cemetery, his crackling footsteps practically the only sound, when he caught a soft noise away to his right.

He stopped, set the barrow down, pushed his black, thick-framed glasses further up his nose and peered into the darkness.

It was about twenty minutes after six. The cemetery closed at six, and was usually cleared fifteen minutes before that, so there shouldn't be anyone left around except perhaps the odd member of staff. The only reason Nicolas himself was still here was that he had wanted to finish laying in the new bed of Michaelmas daisies and pink and white Salvias that had occupied his entire afternoon.

As he squinted into the jumbled silhouettes of tombstones and sepulchers, crypts, mausoleums and monuments, he played the sound back through his mind. It had been a brief sort of *scratching* sound, much like a rake being dragged over hard ground.

He rubbed uncertainly at his stubbled jowl, then called, 'Hello?'

His voice sounded louder in the heavy silence than it actually was. Not that the early evening was exactly *silent* as such, anyway. In the distance he could hear the traffic in the Rue des Pyrénées while, closer to hand, a cool, damp wind suddenly sprang up to rattle the branches of the cemetery's six thousand trees.

'Is anyone there?'

There was no answer.

Nicolas pondered his next move. The wisest course would be to head for the administration block and report the matter to security. But he was still a quarter of a mile from the admin block. By the time he got there the trespasser would be long gone.

In any case, there was always the possibility that the trespasser might be no such thing. Now that he thought about it, a funeral had been conducted in that approximate vicinity earlier that afternoon. He remembered seeing a man and his children among the mourners, standing with their heads bowed as the deceased was laid to rest. The children had been sobbing.

Perhaps someone from the group had returned to spend a few final moments in contemplation, and gotten themselves lost in the swelling dusk.

'Hello?' he called again.

Still there was no answer.

Perhaps it was a fox, then. They were everywhere these days.

With a shrug he turned back to the wheelbarrow. If it was a fox, it could wander to its heart's content. If someone was lost, they would eventually find their way to the gate, sound the alarm and be rescued.

But . . .

But what if it was a *vandal?*

It was by no means unusual for people to sneak into the cemetery and deface the graves. It happened time and time again. Security cameras had been installed and guards did what they could to limit the damage, but —

Instead of lifting his barrow and moving off, Nicolas made a decision. This was *his* cemetery. If he let this go and came to work tomorrow morning to find that vandals had been at work, then he would be as guilty as they.

Impulsively, he picked up one of his gardening tools — a dirt-encrusted trowel — and tugged a small flashlight from his overall pocket. He switched on the flashlight and ran its weak beam across the sea of stone before him. Charcoal shadows slipped from right to left, giving the impression that the cemetery was suddenly being deserted by its occupants.

His first sweep revealed nothing. Holding his breath, he swung the flashlight back the other way, slower this time, in a long, deliberate arc —

'*Oh la vache!*'

Eye-shine reflected back at him from a spot about twenty meters away.

He'd been right, then — it was a fox!

But almost as soon as he thought it, he corrected himself. No . . . that eye-shine . . . it was too high up for a fox. In fact, it was roughly at the height of a short man.

And it was blood-red — or was that nothing more than a trick of the light?

Deciding that, just this once, he was going to assert himself, he stepped onto the grass verge and then in among all the monuments. With as much authority as he could muster he called, 'You, there! Are you lost? The cemetery's closed and you have no business here!'

Still there came no response.

He picked his way deeper between the jumble of headstones. Off to his left a short way he noticed the silhouette of a derelict, scaled-down mausoleum, complete with some sort of decorative figure crouching on its flat roof with huge wings folded back. It reminded Nicolas that there was no shortage of bizarre monuments to be found among all the unsung works of art.

Without warning he caught a stir of movement in the darkness ahead, just beyond the beam of his flashlight. Pulse racing now, he hurried forward, belly bouncing, and raised the torch a little, stabbing it forward as if it were a weapon.

And there, caught in the beam no more than five meters in front of him —

His first thought was that it was a man bending down before the mound of packed dirt that marked the fresh grave. The grieving husband, perhaps, unable to come to terms with his loss?

'*M'sieur* — ' he began.

But then Nicolas saw the wider picture. He realized suddenly that much of the dirt had been dug up and cast carelessly aside; that the coffin had already been dragged half out of its plot. He saw that the man had already managed to wrench back the lid, breaking the hermetic seal and exposing the body within, and was —

— was —

— *was using his teeth to tear a strip of flesh from one of its cold, dead arms.*

Shock whacked Nicolas in the stomach and for one vital moment wiped all coherent thought from his mind. Then —

What . . . ?

WHAT?

What is that?

Disturbed, the thing he had taken to be a man turned impossibly fast at the waist and glared at him, revealing broken yellow teeth that glistened redly in the light as his lips peeled back in a snarl.

It was then that Nicolas realized this was no man.

It was something very different.

Something much . . . *worse.*

It stood about five feet in height, its thick, scaled body bent forward slightly on short, warped legs. Its red eyes were two round balls that bulged from lidless sockets, much like those of a chameleon. Its nose was flat and its nostrils flared. Three small horns jutted from his sloping forehead, one above each eye and the third standing proud between them, and around its misshapen head flew a gauzy curtain of tiny, buzzing flies.

The thing, whatever it was, appeared almost to have been fashioned from dry gray clay.

It gave voice to a furious hiss and then lunged at him, but by then Nicolas was turning, lurching off into the darkness, desperately determined to outrun it.

He stumble-ran five meters, little whimpering sounds spilling from between his lips, before he realized he was going in the wrong direction, blundering even deeper into this field of the dead. Frantically he changed course, his breathing loud in his ears, as was the sound —

Oh no —

As was the sound of pursuit.

He fumbled with the flashlight, trying to turn it off because it was telling that . . . that *thing* . . . exactly where he was. When his thumb refused to cooperate he flung the flashlight away from him. It shattered and went out.

Reckless now, he continued on, banging his shins on low monuments, grazing himself as he darted between leaning headstones.

Where was he? Where was the path?

Suddenly he tripped, went straight down and knocked his head on the corner of a headstone. The pain slashed through him; he swore, sprang back up and kept running —

A taloned claw fastened on his right shoulder, stopping him in his tracks, twisting him around.

His mouth dropped open. He stared wide-eyed into the face of . . . of . . .

What was it? Some sort of ghoul? A body-snatcher?

The thing's red gaze burned into him, and there in the rising moonlight it seemed almost to smile as if in anticipation of this man-meal served hot instead of cold.

Then —

Nicolas smashed it in the face with his trowel, and taken by surprise the stubby gray monster reeled sideways.

Not waiting for it to recover, Nicolas turned and ran on, hopping over floral displays and cursing himself for not being fitter, always doing his best to follow an imaginary half-circle that would take him back to the path.

A shushing sound made his risk a look over one shoulder. He saw the silhouette of that . . . that monstrosity perhaps ten meters behind him, that it was weaving between all the headstones, striding purposefully after him, not rushing, apparently seeing no need to rush.

Ahead, the moonlight showed him the path, and his wheelbarrow. Once he was on solid ground and no longer encumbered by obstacles, he might just be able to outrace his pursuer.

He surged back past the derelict mausoleum with the angel crouching on its flat roof.

But in his haste he did not realize that the 'angel' had *disappeared*.

He slipped off the verge and onto the path. A pitiful sob of gratitude spilled from his mouth. He slipped a little, almost lost his balance, caught it just at the last second and then looked around frantically to get his bearings.

In the same moment there came a

papery rustle behind him, and something like a stray breeze ruffled his short black hair.

Already freaked out, he yelped and he turned, expecting to see —

But it *wasn't* that thing he had seen tearing flesh off the dead woman's exposed arm.

It was worse than that.

He reared back from the tall, thin form that now confronted him. Like that other nightmare, this one was also naked, its pocked gray skin stretched drum-tight over a near skeletal frame. It had long arms, long legs, and a long neck upon which sat a bald, sore-covered head with pointed ears. It had no eyes as we know them, only sickly, pus-yellow cavities, and as it cackled it revealed long, needle-sharp teeth that looked decayed and slimy.

As it laughed at his terror, its huge, thin, membranous wings folded in and flat to its back.

With a scream Nicolas did the only thing he could — he stabbed the . . . the *thing* . . . in chest with his trowel.

The blade of the trowel tore through

the creature's thin skin like a knife tearing through muslin. A puff of dust clouded from the wound, but nothing else, no blood, no liquid of any kind —

The thing looked down at him from its yellow, runny eyes. It stood at least two and a half meters tall, and dwarfed him.

It reached up and plucked the trowel out of its seemingly hollow chest, then tossed the implement aside.

A low, gurgling snarl made Nicolas tear his unbelieving eyes away from the winged thing. Its companion, the squat, horned flesh-eating creature that looked as if it had been fashioned out of clay, stamped out onto the path, came toward him in something that approximated an unstoppable march, then closed the claws of its right hand around his windpipe, effectively stifling further screams.

The thing looked at him through its gauze of buzzing flies and once again seemed almost to . . .

. . . to *smile*.

Its talons tightened, sealing his trachea. And as the shadows began to close in around him, Nicolas decided that his mother had been right. If this was how it was to end for him, then life really *was* a rather disappointing business.

There was a sudden mulching of bone, a squeezing and popping of compressed flesh, and then all thought ceased.

Blood ran down over the horned thing's claws.

Skarasis, cannibal brother of Milaroth, let Nicolas drop to the ground, then used his long, forked tongue to lick the blood appreciatively from his long, hooked nails. And while Amorion, the third of Milaroth's brothers, watched, the creature dropped to his knees before the body and began to feast.

10

The Air France Boeing 777-200 took off from Charles de Gaulle's Runway One twenty minutes behind schedule. It climbed gracefully into the stormy evening sky, its navigation lights twinkling and shrinking with every passing second.

Danielle watched until it was completely lost to sight, then said, '*Merçi.*' Touching Archer's arm, she added, 'I know you have made the right decision.'

Hoping but by no means convinced that she was right, Archer turned away from the Terminal One departure hall window.

The girl had stayed with him all day, apparently as reluctant to say goodbye to him as he'd been to hear it. She'd assured him that she wouldn't mention Palden again, or what they'd experienced the night before, and to his surprise she'd been as good as her word.

'But . . . I won't see you again, will I?'

she'd added sadly. 'After you leave, I mean?'

He shook his head.

She was silent for a long moment, before finally nodding to herself and announcing, 'Then we will take *what* we can, *while* we can.'

Naïvely, and with more than a dash of panic, he thought, *We're going to bump fuzzies.*

'Wh-what do you mean?' he asked.

'Come on,' she said. 'I'll show you.'

And she did.

She took him to the Musée D'Orsay and showed him works of art by the likes of Monet, Renoir and Toulouse-Lautrec. She took him to Montmartre, from there through the Marais, with its ribbon-thin cobbled streets and quaintly Jewish restaurants, and on along the Canal Saint-Martin. And finally, as the afternoon began to wane, they visited the Île-De-France, the Place des Abbesses and the Square Jehan-Rictus, where lovers traditionally scratch their initials on padlocks and attach them to the wire mesh parapets of the Pont des Arts as a symbol of their undying love.

He wished he could have enjoyed it to the full, but he was too preoccupied for that. All he could do was look at the people around them and envy them their ignorance of life's dark side, their ability to concentrate on their own affairs and not have to weigh the consequences of their every action before taking it. Just for once he wanted *not* to be so constantly troubled. But that option had never been open to him . . . and perhaps it never would be.

At last Danielle checked the new watch she'd bought to replace the one that had been ruined by its immersion in the Seine, then looked up at him and said regretfully, 'Well . . . I suppose we had better get you to the airport now, otherwise you'll miss your flight.'

He wondered if she was hoping he would relent and say that he'd changed his mind, that she had changed it for him, and he would go and do his best to slay Milaroth and his kin.

He didn't.

They took a taxi back to his hotel and

he collected his cross-body bag and checked out. The same taxi sped them out of the city toward Charles de Gaulle Airport. He checked in, and then they found seats and waited in silence for his flight to be called.

'Whatever happens,' she said softly when the announcement finally echoed through the public address system, 'I will never forget you, Archer. How you saved me last night.'

He climbed to his feet and scooped up his bag, not really knowing what to tell her.

'I hope you find your family,' she said, and standing alongside him, she reached up to plant a dainty kiss on his cheek. 'That you have a happy ending.'

He looked down at her. There was no sarcasm in her sentiment. She really *meant* it.

Then, almost before he realized it, he said, 'I can't do it.'

She looked at him. *'Excusez-moi?'*

'You know I can't,' he said irritably. 'Palden knows I can't. The only person who didn't know it was me — until now.'

'I don't under — '

'Don't you?'

Emotion fluttered across her face, transforming her expression, softening it. 'You'll help him?' she said, her voice holding a kind of wonder. 'You will kill these demons?'

'I'll *try*.'

He tried also not to acknowledge the surge of relief his decision sent through him. 'But then I'm through,' he added. 'And I mean it, this time.'

★　★　★

Now, as they drove back toward the night-dark city, the sky filled with bulky, ominous clouds as purple as fresh bruises.

The sudden change in the weather confirmed what Archer already suspected — that Palden planned to lure Milaroth and his siblings to the Eiffel Tower and when the moment was right summon an electrical charge from the storm he was even now calling up to effectively turn the Tower into an enormous arc furnace in which to obliterate them.

It was a risky plan, the plan of a desperate man who no longer had sufficient strength to slay his enemies by spells alone, a man who was willing to sacrifice his own life so long as it meant destroying those of Mankind's foes.

It put Archer to shame.

Around them, the temperature dropped perceptibly.

The taxi drew to a halt, they climbed out and Archer told the driver to wait. Sleet spat at them and a raw blast of Arctic air howled between the tower's latticework of steel girders, imitating the wails of lost spirits.

'Where's Palden?' asked Danielle, looking around fearfully.

Archer lifted his eyes to the tower. Invisible to all but those who knew what to look for, a shimmering aura danced and sparkled around the summit.

'Up there,' he said.

'He can't be. It's after midnight. The tower's been closed for almost an hour.'

'He's up there,' Archer said with certainty.

'But . . . how? I mean, how was it no one in authority saw him and told him to leave?'

'I don't know. There's a lot about that man I don't know yet. But I know he's up there right now, summoning this storm — and luring them in.' He looked down at her, said tenderly, 'Go home now, Danielle. And pray to whichever god you believe in.'

'What about you?' she asked.

Every time sleet struck her face, her eyelids flickered.

'I've got some demons to slay,' he said — and smiled.

Impulsively she kissed him again, and again the urgent press of her lips was exhilarating. Then he pulled away from her, watched her climb back into the taxi and drive away.

She waved at him from the rear window. He raised one hand and waved back. Then the taxi turned a corner and was lost to sight, and he knew with a wrench of pure emotion that he would never see her again.

Firming his jaw, he turned and headed

for one of the tower's four splayed legs at a trot.

When he reached it, he began to climb. And he made it look *easy*.

In the distance, thunder rumbled and lightning flickered restlessly across the sky. Ignoring it, Archer kept moving, focusing, stretching, springing when he had to, but always finding hand- and foot-holds that would take him ever higher.

Below him lay the leafy parkland of the Champ de Mars, plunged into near-darkness now, and the brightly-lit splendor of the Trocadèro fountains. To the north he could just about make out the Musée de la Marine.

An icy wind shook the city's many trees and made their branches rattle.

Higher he went, climbing like a human spider. Once he passed the first floor restaurant, the angle of his ascent grew ever steeper and the strain began to tell on his arms, his back, his legs. It began to rain more heavily, turning each enormous pig-iron girder even more slippery, making the climb ever more treacherous, but Archer never once slowed down.

After what seemed like forever he reached the second level and went higher, past the Jules Verne Restaurant, scaling the 324-meter tower more like a ladder now, until a sense of unease gripped him tight and refused to let go.

All at once he stopped, and heeding his instincts glanced back over one shoulder.

At first he didn't see anything.

Then —

Something far, far below had just started climbing the tower beneath him, scurrying up in his wake.

Correction.

Two somethings.

Almost at the same moment his attention was taken by a peculiar, dry rustling sound somewhere behind him. As it came closer it grew increasingly frenzied.

Then, seemingly right out of nowhere, two long-fingered hands latched onto his shoulders. Their claws punctured his flesh and he felt the sudden, sticky-warm splash of blood run down his back and chest. Something yanked him away from his perch; he lost his grip on the girder and before he knew it, he found himself suspended in mid-air, wind-blown and rain-lashed.

Behind and a little above him, something cackled. It was an odd, papery, malicious sound. Archer twisted and looked up over one painful shoulder, already knowing what he was going to see — Milaroth's brother, Amorion.

More lightning flared, illuminating the demon.

He was tall and cadaverous, his soulless body as hollow as his loveless heart, with his round, sore-covered head, his overlong arms and legs, and his paper-thin, membranous wings.

The wings were beating now, almost so hummingbird-fast that it was impossible to see them, and the demon himself was crowing at Archer's desperate attempts to grab for the relative safety of the tower.

Amorion flew a little higher, a little further away from the tower . . . and then let him go.

Helpless to save himself, Archer plunged toward the ground.

At the last moment he snatched wildly at one of Amorion's skinny ankles and held firm. His weight, slight as it was, was enough to make the winged one lurch sickeningly down and to one side. The creature's pus-filled eyes narrowed on him; he showed his long, needle-sharp teeth in a furious hiss and tried to kick him loose.

Still Archer held tight, then started swinging himself like a pendulum to drag the fluttering creature above him back toward the tower.

Amorion shrieked, reached down, and tried to knock him loose. Archer ignored him as best he could and dodged and ducked to avoid the flailing claws, all the time swinging on the demon's leg to drag it closer to the tower.

Unfortunately, the tower was still three meters away.

Something, one of the things climbing the tower below him, suddenly flashed past him and kept climbing.

Thinking fast, Archer yelled, *'Carlem! Koas! Cameerinthum! Amorion!'*

The winged demon's face slackened as

146

Archer spoke the words, his expression of evil swiftly replaced by one of horror as his skin began to smolder and little patches of fire started igniting all over his body.

Again Archer swung from the thin, kicking leg, but now Amorion was otherwise occupied with the tiny, flickering fires that were erupting all over him, the flames curiously bright, and impervious to the driving rain.

Three meters dropped to two, and still Amorion screamed and screeched and tried to kick him loose. But now Archer was close enough to risk the leap he'd been planning to make, and all at once he let go of the demon's ankle and sprang for the nearest girder.

He hit hard, waking fresh pain in his already-tender ribs, but gripped and held.

A second later Amorion grabbed at him again, wings still beating furiously, little patches of flame still erupting all over him. He tugged again, determined to pluck Archer from the structure.

Archer threw an awkward punch back at the demon and missed. Amorion squeezed harder, his claws sinking deeper into the bleeding meat of Archer's shoulders.

Again Archer bawled the spell. *'Carlem! Koas! Cameerinthum! Amorion!'*

And now even more fingers of fire started popping through the demon's cratered skin. One pointed ear began to smoke and then abruptly burst into flame. Amorion screamed as the flames continued to grow and spread and slowly, steadily consume him.

The demon gave one final tug at Archer, and then, with a banshee wail, his claws loosened and Amorion began to tumble end over end back toward the ground, the flames fairly feasting on him now.

But that final tug had been enough.

Archer lost his grip on the girder and fell.

He fell perhaps five meters before managing to catch hold of another girder and halt his downward plunge. The effort almost tore his arm from its socket and a fierce jag of white-hot pain speared through him, but somehow he held on. He *had* to.

Far, far below him, Amorion hit the ground and burst apart, sparks flying up from all that remained of his charred-black corpse.

But the other thing, the thing Archer now identified as Skarasis, was still dragging himself hand over hand up the tower, coming closer with every step.

Which must mean that the figure that had passed him as he fought with Amorion was Milaroth.

Whipped by rain, Archer laced one arm around the girder and looked back down at the abomination that was suddenly no more than ten meters below him: Skarasis, the Feaster-on-Flesh, squat and chunky in his gray, scaled skin, with a gauze of small flies constantly buzzing around his horned head, and two blood-red balls for eyes, each one capable of independent movement.

Archer stared down at the apparition, feeling the absolute, unadulterated evil belching off him in great malevolent waves. Skarasis glared back at him, then opened his mouth, revealed the large, decaying yellow teeth with which he had consumed a million human meals, and hissed at him.

Swallowing hard, Archer set himself and cried, *'By the Creativity of the Maiden this Spell was Written . . . '*

Skarasis bellowed at him and started climbing again, higher, faster —

' . . . *Sustained by the Unending Energy of the Mother —* '

Closer, closer, growling, snarling . . .

Archer jabbed his right hand toward the demon, freezing him in his tracks. *'The Crone of Great Power dissolves your Unwanted Form, and Banishes you from This Place Forever More —* '

Skarasis lunged forward and reached for him. Archer dodged, stared him straight in the eye and cried, *'As It Will, So Mote It Be!'*

Skarasis screamed — and with shocking speed his every festering bone seemed suddenly to just *vanish*, and without any support, what was left of him simply caved in on itself and toppled loosely to the earth.

11

Archer clung to the tower, breathing hard. For a moment the world began to tilt around him. He swallowed again and tried to push the nausea away. *You've slain three of them*, he thought. *There's only one left to kill. You can do this.*

Doggedly he started climbing again, as the storm continued to flash and growl around him. Seen from this vantage, Paris looked more like a diorama, its miniature streets deserted and made as if to shine by the constant slam of freezing rain.

At last he reached the overhang at the top of the tower. He felt drained. But directly above him now he would find Palden and Milaroth, and then he would finish this once and for all.

His arms feeling more like lead weights, he picked a path through the shadowy network of girders beneath the observation platform until he reached the empty elevator shaft. Here he forced his pupils to expand until he could see, as clear as day, the elevator cables hanging side by side like sleeping snakes.

He was just about to leap for the stoutest one when he heard a sound somewhere up above.

A long, low, drawn-out and thoroughly evil *snarl*

He froze.

And then —

Palden's voice: *'I ask for the God and Goddess to assist me in banishing this force and eliminating its destructiveness . . . '*

Once more Archer's jaw set hard. Palden must have seen or sensed him destroy Amorion and Skarasis, and abandoned his plan to turn the tower into an arc furnace. Now that only Milaroth remained, he was attempting to slay him with a spell. Whether or not he had enough strength to make it work remained to be seen.

Recklessly Archer made his leap, caught the thickest of the elevator cables, swung to and fro, to and fro . . . then started climbing.

Palden's voice, echoing down the shaft, grew steadily louder. *'In the name of the Lord and the Lady, I charge you to serve me within this circle. I clear you of all former influences and energies that you may be fit for the workings of Magic herein.'*

And Milaroth, still snarling, the ponderous *thump, thump* of the demon as he stamped around the observation platform overhead, with Palden constantly backing away, backing away, trying to make the magic work.

Muscles flexing and straining now, Archer climbed higher, higher . . .

'Thou creature of paper. By paper made, by paper changed. So mote it be!'

The incantation was followed by a violent rush of sound, a clanging of something heavy striking wire mesh.

Archer came level with the closed elevator doors, once more swung himself back and forth like a pendulum, reached out with one hand, and grabbed at the narrow join between the two sliding doors. At the same time he managed to catch the tips of his sneakered feet on the thin ledge.

Urgently he set to work, trying to prise the doors open. Stubbornly, they remained shut tight.

Open . . . open . . .

He felt his nails tearing at the roots but ignored the pain. All that mattered now was finishing this — finishing Milaroth and beginning his search for his sister Gadreel . . .

Without warning the elevator doors yielded and Archer lurched out onto a wide observation platform that ran around the central elevator shaft and staircase. The platform was fenced in overhead with some sort of thick wire mesh. He saw that a great chunk of it had been wrenched out of shape — presumably where Milaroth had gained access.

On the far side of the platform he heard Palden yell, *'Blazing force of cleansing fire, Help me in this rite. By air — '*

The chant ended abruptly.

Too abruptly.

Summoning his last reserves of energy,

Archer sprinted around the platform until he saw Milaroth looming over Palden, holding the black man as if he were weightless.

Palden was semi-conscious, bleeding from the forehead, looking anything but stylish now.

As Archer watched, Milaroth shook his head to detach his jaw; his mouth opened impossibly wide . . .

He was going to bite Palden's head off.

Archer's own mouth yanked wide, he screamed Milaroth's name, and even as the demon began to turn —

Archer left the ground and leapt at him, one foot slamming the creature hard in the small of his spiny back.

Milaroth lurched forward, off-balance. He dropped Palden, shook his head to reattach his jaw and twisted around to face this new threat.

Recognizing Archer, realizing that Archer's presence here meant that his brothers had failed in their mission to destroy him and had themselves been destroyed instead, he came forward, quickly slashing his arms from side to side. Archer backed up, ducked, darted back in, and punched the demon wrist-deep in his stomach.

With a growl, Milaroth launched a swinging backhander. It grazed Archer's forehead and with a metallic *clangggg* he fell back against the platform railings.

Milaroth came after him, and Archer kept retreating, blocking blows, launching blows of his own whenever an opportunity presented itself.

Suddenly he tucked himself in beneath those flailing arms, twisted, elbowed Milaroth repeatedly in his armored stomach, brought his right hand up in a savage backhand strike to the creature's face, turned again, launched a straight-leg kick to the sternum, and sent Milaroth staggering back.

Staring Milaroth directly in the face, he cried breathlessly, '*By air and earth, water and fire, So be you bound With this rite, Your power takes flight, Sky and sea, Keep harm from me, Cord go round, Power be bound. Your negativity will no longer come my way!*'

Milaroth screamed, his tail lashing

furiously one way, then the other.

'From henceforth, your power over me is banished!' yelled Archer.

And then he stopped.

Palden, scrambling back to his feet in the background, frowned and thought, *What the hell's he doin'? Just finish the damn' ritual and kill that sonofabitch!*

Milaroth swayed, his muddy red eyes already dimming.

But Archer looked past him, straight at Palden.

And *smiled*.

'*You* softened him up,' he called. '*You* finish him off.'

Palden stared at him, not quite sure he'd heard right.

'Go ahead,' called Archer, suddenly a little crazy with all he'd just been through, and all that he had just survived. 'Have this one on me, Glorious One!'

Hardly believing Archer's gall, Palden cleared his throat, rubbed his hands, and enjoying the moment to the full bellowed at the top of his lungs, *'So Mote it Be!'*

What happened next was hard to describe.

Milaroth seemed to turn inside-out,

then back again. It happened again almost immediately; he became so much red meat and raw white bone, then turned outside-in again.

It happened twice more, three times, five, nine, a dozen, again, again, again.

Inside out and back, inside out and back —

Faster, faster, faster —

Milaroth screeched —

— and then burst apart like a pin-pricked balloon.

Red meat and black blood slapped and spattered everywhere. The rain slowly but steadily began to wash it away.

Soon only two figures occupied the observation platform where so recently there had been three.

'Well,' Palden managed after a few moments, 'you sure took your time showin' up.'

Breathing hard, Archer glared at him. 'Don't make me sorry I saved your life, Palden.'

'Saved my — ? Hey, wait a *minute!* You didn't save my life, Champ! What you jus' did was — '

Archer held up one hand to silence him. 'I know, I know ... on-the-job training, right?'

Palden's teeth flared whitely in a grin. 'Got it in one.'

He thought there might be hope for this kid yet.

As the last few chunks of demon-meat dissolved in the cleansing rain, he took out his cigarettes, tucked one between his lips, cupped it from the downpour and lit it. Then, without looking at Archer, he said quietly, 'She told you everythin', right? The girl, Danielle?'

He nodded tiredly. 'Yes.'

'So now you know all about your sister.'

'Yes.'

'Well, I won't rest until I find her, Champ.'

'That's funny,' Archer said quietly. 'Neither will I.'

'All right. So let's cut us a deal.'

'What kind of deal?'

'We stand a better chance of findin' her if we work together, right?'

'I suppose.'

'So what say we start over tomorrow? Me an' you? Pullin' together? Master an' student?'

Archer looked out over the sleeping city. 'I think we may have to revise that 'master and student' bit,' he said. 'But tomorrow . . . tomorrow sounds good.'

Suddenly he cracked another exhausted smile.

'Now let's get out of here,' he said. 'I might be a Demon-Slayer, Palden, but I think I've slain enough demons for one day, don't you?'

THE END